ALL'S FAIR
AND OTHER CALIFORNIA STORIES

ALL'S FAIR

AND OTHER CALIFORNIA STORIES

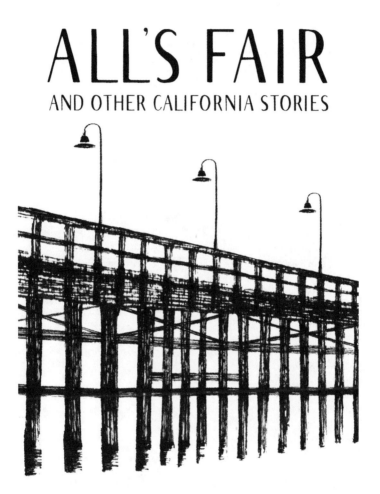

LINDA FEYDER

SHE WRITES PRESS

Published 2021
Printed in the United States of America
Print ISBN: 978-1-64742-199-1
E-ISBN: 978-1-64742-200-4
Library of Congress Control Number: 2021909574

For information, address:
She Writes Press
1569 Solano Ave #546
Berkeley, CA 94707

Interior design by Tabitha Lahr

She Writes Press is a division of SparkPoint Studio, LLC.

To Beatrice, my mom and first reader

Author's Note

The stories in this collection were originally published in *The Alembic*; *Latina: Women's Voices from the Borderlands*; *Hispanic* magazine; *The Americas*; *Words*; *In Other Words: Literature by Latinas of the United States*; and *riverSedge*.

Contents

All's Fair

When Brian knocked on the door, Joyce jumped from her chair in a panic. Her husband, Louis, had trouble falling asleep at night, so she rushed to answer it before Brian knocked again and awakened him. Reading glasses shot off her nose and struck her chest where they hung from a chain. Of course it was Brian. He always knocked hard and slid his side against the door. Twelve years old, the son of the superintendent, Brian seemed much younger to her—probably because he was an albino.

"What is it, Brian?" she whispered anxiously, opening the door.

"I wanna show you something. Hurry!"

"Shh. Louis is asleep."

"Come on! You'll miss it!"

"What is it?"

Never expect an answer to that question, she thought. She'd asked it many times, only to follow him through the condominium complex to the recesses of the redwood pool shed, the game room, or the garage where the restored Studebaker was parked. Once, it had been to see Mrs. Becker's bra, which he had stretched across the Ping-Pong table like a net; another time, to watch two green crickets mating.

But it was dark out and she was tired and ready for bed. It had been a trying day with Louis. First, he wouldn't go out for some fresh air. "*Fresh* air. Who needs *fresh* air!" he'd said with his mimicking voice, the one she'd hated in the old days, when they could have equal fights. Then he wouldn't eat the dinner she'd cooked. Baked chicken with potatoes and carrots. The skin removed. Everything low-fat and as the doctor had directed. All of this was aggravated by the night before. He had refused to turn off CNN. She'd struggled to block out news of the Ebola virus in Zaire, the closing of Pennsylvania Avenue to detonating trucks. The clock had read 2:00 a.m. "I can't sleep. I'm still watching it," he'd said. She could have gotten up and turned it off, and there would, of course, have been nothing he could do.

These thoughts were common lately. She knew it. Ones in which she defied her immobile husband, with enormous pleasure, and the fantasies troubled her. In one, she left him in the bath-tub, say, an extra half hour when he complained about the water temperature, which she could never get quite right. Or she had a van service whisk him straight to the barber when he pronounced only she could cut his hair.

How, then, could she explain her compassion the last time she had caught him struggling to pull up his pants? He had been a tall, big-boned man, an administrator at the city college for some thirty years. Once a year, a handful of graduating students came over for a curry dish he'd cook himself. He had enjoyed lengthy squash games and reading political biographies on a Central Park bench. And now retired to this? She felt the urge to protect him, to wrap her arms around his shrinking frame, as she might have done when their daughter, Carol, was young and scraped her knee on a subway grate.

"Let me help you, Lou," she would say, reaching for the waist of his pants.

He'd look up, embarrassed to be caught, and say, "I'll ask when I need your help."

Now, here stood Brian with his little albino demands. She hated herself for thinking this. *How cruel, cruel.* She should follow him. She should indulge his wishes because life had dealt him a pitiless blow, one colorless and pale, and she had seen it hit her husband too, reducing him to a bedridden tyrant. *No, I don't mean that.* She must, she told herself, be patient.

Joyce slid her feet into the gardening clogs she kept beside the door. Each unit in the complex came with a five-by-seven plot for gardening, and, though she had never gardened before, she took to it with a special kind of vengeance. She learned about dirts, mulches, and fertilizers. She bought a wicker work basket from a gardener's catalog and filled it with little wooden-handled tools she had no idea how to use—hoe knife, cultivator, dibble, and trowel.

She didn't close the door all the way, intending to make it quick. The concrete walk sounded beneath her clogs. It was dark out. She followed the cap of pure white hair. Every once in a while, Brian glanced over his shoulder to make sure she was still there, his pale eyes like two pieces of chalk.

Outside, the vast desert sky stretched above, giving her a feeling of vertigo if she stared at it for too long. She still wasn't used to this sky and longed for tall buildings to anchor her. She and Louis had moved here, to Palm Desert, California, from Manhattan for the warm, arid weather his doctor recommended. Years of things had been packed in boxes and moved to a place that made them look shabby in the intense light. Their collection of city landscape paintings suddenly looked dreary and old-fashioned. Louis's large leather chair sagged beneath the tall windows.

This part of the country was unknown to her. On the map, the region had stretched brown and vast, like a remote outback. They had chosen Palm Desert because it was not far from Los Angeles, where their daughter now lived. The first week they arrived, Carol drove in from LA and took Joyce to every market, pharmacy, shoe-repair shop, and movie theater in town. She remembered that week as a dizzy blur of storefronts and blanched scenery, her daughter like a breathless tour guide working the crowd.

Late fall, she remembered, and the sun had still beamed hotly. Indian summer, she'd been told. The thermometer rarely dipped below ninety degrees. Hot winds had electrified her skirt and splayed her gray hair like a starfish across her forehead. Pavement shimmered. She'd felt like an image on overexposed film, the stark light revealing how she'd let herself go: unplucked eyebrows, the dry skin around her mouth solidifying into wrinkles.

It was a strange thing to transport a life in a gamble for more. The doctor had said many in his condition thrived in this climate for as long as five years.

"Thrived?" Louis had said skeptically, always sensitive to words. He and Joyce had avoided the warm-weather locations. "The silver zones," he liked to call them. Upon retirement, it would have been a bicycle trip through China rather than winters in Florida.

"He's declining," Joyce had told Carol over the phone just before they decided to move. Nearly forty years of accumulation in the closets and drawers. Matchbooks, like travel diaries, would fall out of the corners, listing where they had been and where they had wished to go.

"Is it worth it?" Carol had asked. Meaning, *Will he really get three to five years more?*

Carol had adjusted well to her new life on the West Coast. In three years, she had been promoted to junior partner, her New York resolve impressing the firm. She had made friends. She had traded some of her rigor for a new fluidity, yet she still had a knack for the naked question.

"You'd uproot your entire life," she'd said. "Friends, neighborhood, doctors—your routine. Are you sure, Mom?"

What Joyce knew she'd miss were people on the street. It would be different from New York. In the city, she often made conversation with strangers. They would talk about anything: the weather, food, local news. Once, engrossed in a conversation with a German tourist, she had missed her train stop.

Surprisingly, though, what she'd already missed most was no longer there to leave. The texture rather than the fabric. The way things were done rather than the actual things. She missed the cheerful, efficient way Louis had unfolded the card table rather than the weekly bridge game with Don and Beryl. The eager way his hands had riffled through the Sunday *Times*, not the thick newspaper they hauled to the Polish diner as part of their weekly ritual. She missed the mornings of bumping into his large body in their small kitchen, a nuisance she now understood as a tactile pleasure.

So it was Palm Desert or the removal of a small hope, and Joyce chose the former, though she nearly cried when the movers came for the boxes, when their friends said their goodbyes, veiled in comforting phrases that promised unexpected visits and amusing letters.

Joyce took Louis for a stroll while Carol opened the late-to-arrive boxes crammed in their new condominium.

"An expansive golf course view," the real estate agent had said eagerly, as if their condominium windows would open onto a God-given landscape. Odd little rock and cactus gardens ornamented the complex. She couldn't get used to seeing cacti in a garden; they were ugly, prickly things that belonged to a desert. Then, she reminded herself, she now lived in the desert.

"Strange," she said to Louis, "to think before irrigation, this desert would have been uninhabitable."

She wasn't sure it was truly habitable now, but she was determined to put a cheerful face on it.

5

Across the walk, they watched their contemporaries cruise the rolling emerald hills in Bermuda shorts and pastel-colored golf carts. Neither of them played golf.

Louis sat in his wheelchair, dressed in the clothes she'd helped him into that morning—a pair of khaki slacks and a navy-blue sweater she now feared was too hot. His chin was still strong and sure. His wavy gray hair had a way of framing his ears that still managed to arouse her.

"When I go," Louis had said, his mouth pulled to one side, the way he did to tell jokes, "you should get out of here."

It was then that she felt the first urge to push his wheelchair into the sand pit. *We've come all this way, and this is all the hope you can muster?* The idea of defying him, of imagining him face-down in the sand, gave her a sudden moment of relief. Since they'd moved, an alarming variety of these fantasies had given her relief. But she stamped them down. Stamp, stamp. *How cruel. How cruel.* Racked with guilt, she would spend an extra half hour planting the goldfinks she'd kept waiting in their symmetrical plastic containers. She had read in a gardening book, "Ordinary garden soil and full sun. Rich soil is to be avoided."

"Where are you going, Brian?"

He threaded her down the narrow walk toward the golf course. "Williamson's back," he called over his shoulder, shooting a finger at the lighted window across the walk. He knew the complex like the veins peering through the translucent skin of his hands. Comings and goings. This place his little fiefdom, she thought, with mounting affection.

"He collects things," Brian said. "Butterflies with gnarly wings. Rusted corkscrews. I'll show you sometime if you want."

How did we all end up here? she wondered. *This odd assortment? This eclectic bunch?* Brian's family had moved from Pennsylvania a year before she and Louis had. Brian's parents shared the job of superintendent for the complex, which meant that his mother, who seemed to have more business sense, dealt with the finances and his father tended to repairs.

The first time she met Brian, she was standing outside the Spanish-tiled condominiums, grocery bags hanging from her arms. Several boys circled around him, hassling Brian about his baseball cap. He always wore it in the daytime, pulling it conspicuously low to shield his pink eyes, so he appeared to walk with his nose hooked to the bill. His pure white hair peeked out along the cap's edges.

One large boy yanked the cap off his head, mimicking Brian's discomfort in the sun. The boy withered to the ground. "I'm melting! I'm melting!" he taunted.

Brian groped again and again for the cap, fumbling like an injured bird. He reached like Louis did now for a glass of water on the nightstand, determined yet weak. Then he stepped back when a bright stroke of sun hit his pale eyes.

"Give him the cap back!" she yelled. "Give it to him now!"

The grocery bags slid from her arms. She ran across the wide, empty street, waving her hands as if shooing flies. The boys chuckled. They pinched Brian's hot white cheek, then tossed the cap into a cactus garden and swaggered away, bouncing and laughing, calling back, "The albino's got a bodyguard. Look at that! Whee-hee! Better bring Grandma to school tomorrow."

Brian strained to pluck his cap out of the cactus. He pricked his arm, finally drew the cap out, then slapped it across his knee to shake out any needles.

"Are you all right?" she said, her voice still pitched high from the excitement.

He regarded her with a flushed, impatient look. *The chagrin of the weak,* Joyce thought. His T-shirt was bunched up in the middle, so his white stomach glared in the hot sun.

"What're you doing here?" he asked.

She collected herself and gestured toward his cap, hanging like a fallen bird in his hand.

"I don't need your help," he said, hurling the cap into the center of the street. "You can have it if you want." And then he ran.

Linked from that moment on, she thought now, following his bright, capless hair in the darkness, by his confusion after that humiliating afternoon. Shame and anger, she knew—her husband waving her away when she rushed to help him out of bed—were unidentified friends. Later, Brian came to her door, the cap returned to his hands, to begin the first day of their new friendship. He took her that day to see Mrs. Goldenbaum's cross-eyed tabby cat. His role from then on would be to amuse her, to find things worthy of her attention.

Or had it been *his* amusement with what he could get her to do?

He was a peculiar child with a never-ending supply of fascinations. *Why am I doing this? I'm tired and it's late.* No more walks to his little show-and-tells, she decided. No more caterpillars or rusted corkscrews.

Brian stopped and whirled around on his toes. The path light shone down on his head so his hair glowed white-blue.

"Wanna know where we're going?" he teased. He spun back around and continued walking.

"Yes, I do." She stopped, her hands on her waist.

"Just a little more," he pleaded, crouching and tugging on his pants at the knees.

Then, to keep her amused, he rubbed his palms together just below his nose, occasionally flicking at them with his starkly red tongue. His eyes darted back and forth.

"What am I?" he asked.

"Heaven knows," she said, a grin rising that she was powerless to control. This odd boy. Yes, it was why she liked him so much.

8

"A fly!" he said, whirling back around.

She followed him over a grassy knoll, then down to a cement drainage ditch that cut across the golf course like a scar. He straddled the ditch, his two sneakers hobbling its sides. Joyce wasn't about to attempt the ditch in her clogs, so she walked beside it, watching Brian bounce from side to side, his pace quickening, eyes lowered to the cement.

She began to enjoy the walk. The air finally cooled, and tall palm trees fanned in the breeze. The grass felt soft and smelled sweet beneath her. She heard Brian's quick, short breaths keeping rhythm with his feet.

Sweet, clever boy. She was suddenly glad to follow him. She remembered the time, several weeks after the boys had harassed him, when she'd come home to find Brian crouched beneath the coffee table in her living room.

"We're playing hide-and-seek," he'd whispered.

She'd looked toward the hallway, confused. She had half anticipated Louis to walk into the room. "Let's go see a show," she might have said. Or, "Guess who I ran into on the train?" Deep down, she knew it wasn't true—his condition had worsened—yet for that moment she had a child's freedom from the hard facts.

"You're under the coffee table!" Louis had called from his bed.

Brian rolled out, gripping his sides. "Ahh," he'd said. "No fair. You heard her!"

"All's fair!" Louis's voice had rung through the hall.

As they approached a curve in the ditch, Brian kicked a stone that ricocheted off the cement. *So white.* Why his parents had moved to the desert, she could not understand. Watching him scuttle around the complex in midafternoon, his pale skin exposed to the hot, piercing glare, she had often been inspired to buy him a decent hat, one with a good broad brim. Louis had laughed. "He won't wear that kind of hat, Joyce."

"Why not?"

"The kids wear baseball caps."

She knew he was right. The world worked according to a skewed justice she tried to resist. Why should an albino boy suffer beneath a penetrating sun? Or, for that matter, why should they have moved to a desert so she could watch her husband slowly die?

Brian stopped, his feet planted firmly in the ditch, and lifted his face to listen for something in the distance. Joyce watched his pale eyes, his iridescent skin, so lovely and opaque in the night. She felt an ache in her weak ankle and was about to invite him home for ice cream when she heard something whimper—an animal or a young child?

Brian took off down the ditch. "Hurry!" he yelled. "Look what I found!"

She jerked forward. A small form moved in jagged circles on the other side of the ditch. It whimpered and growled. It cast itself sideways, attempted to run, then flopped onto its side and rolled, its body a tight knot.

"How'd he get out?" Brian shouted.

She strained her eyes to make out the form. A little dog appeared to be caught on its tail, circling madly. Grass flew. It yanked its body around and around until it collapsed, a panting bundle, its dark eyes still with fright.

Brian climbed out of the ditch and moved toward the dog.

"Don't get near it, Brian," she called. "It might bite."

"He won't bite."

"He's caught on something."

"His own tail!" he yelled. He picked up the dog, a twisting ball of white fur. Then he rolled it into the cement ditch. The dog bounced off its left hindquarters. It yelped and writhed harder, ricocheting against the ditch, bounding off one side, rolling to the other. Brian's excitement grew.

"Look! Look!" he yelled. "A pinball!"

He moved toward the ditch, and Joyce suddenly understood that this kid—so delighted by the dog's distress—was the same boy often surrounded by stronger kids, poking and kicking him on the ground.

"Get away!" she shouted.

She slid after him, losing one clog in the ditch. Before Brian grabbed the dog, she smacked his arm away with one quick stroke. She was surprised by her strength, feeling the sting in the palm of her hand.

She reached for the dog. Her fingers searched for the place where it was caught until she found the piece of fishing wire knotted around the tail. The dog yelped. She quickly followed the wire to the collar and then slipped the small knot off the link. The dog sprang from her arms, freed, and scrambled out of the ditch. The wire flailed behind it. She watched it run across the golf course—hot, white, and quick—toward the street, until her eyes could no longer track him in the dark.

She turned an angry face on Brian, who sat sullenly at the edge of the ditch. His eyes were strained red. He scraped his sneaker against the cement.

"Don't you leave," she said, groping for her clog, which lay upside down at the bottom of the ditch. "I want to have a word with you."

She heard more scraping on cement. She rose just as he fled, his sneakers flashing in a bold, bright streak, headed for the stucco walk.

"Brian!" she called. She wanted to run after him, to shake him with the force of her indignation until he came to understand. She grappled with these feelings as she watched him run farther and farther away, beyond her grasp. And then he disappeared.

Joyce crawled out of the ditch and stood to catch her breath. She wiped the lap of her skirt, though there was no dirt on it.

She looked behind her in the direction the dog had run, then in front, and felt the expanse of the foreign landscape around her. If Brian came to her door tomorrow, what would she tell him? That he had surprised her, when the anger she felt was slowly fading?

"I should get back," she said to herself, realizing that she was standing in the middle of a golf course at night.

With one clog in her hand, she hobbled across the grass like a child pretending to limp, feeling, as she went, the dull pleasure of imbalance. She would check on Louis, she thought, then go to her garden, where she'd turn on the porch light and cut the California lilacs, whose exact gardening instructions were somehow reassuring: "Should be pruned hard in spring before new growth appears."

Marta del Ángel

My name is Marta del Ángel. It's a pretty name; I am named after my father's dead sister. In California they call me Mar*tha*, with a tongue stuck to their top front teeth when they come to the "t." It sounds different here, like they're going to spit.

I married an American man I met in a supermarket parking lot. He worked in construction, and when I met him he was sitting in his truck, swallowing beer. I fell in love with his arms; they were golden from the sun, and a thin film of dust glistened on his blond hairs. These are the things of love, my father once told me. "*Cuídese, mi hija.* It only takes one thing."

We rented an apartment in Oxnard, not far from the water. I could hear the bells from the dock and at times a foghorn. The home, I kept it spotless, and my husband never had to wait for his dinner. These are the lessons of my mother. Her kitchen was my classroom, and I learned something. I woke up with the roosters to make fresh cheese for my brothers. My mother tested the coffee before serving it to my father. These things are not uncommon for young women like me.

The second summer of the marriage, my husband said he had a construction job in Arizona, and he never came back. I kept his dinner in the freezer, and on lonely nights I would go to the boats and stare out across the ocean, where on a clear day I could see the dark outlines of the Channel Islands. I liked to think they were the shores of Mexico and the foghorns were her tired sounds, like an old aunt I listened to. My American girlfriend told me my husband was probably just working hard. He'll come home, she said. I wanted to say to her, "You gringas, you are too stupid about men." She took me to the movies. I made her tortas when she came to visit me on her lunch break. I liked her. She wore large, dangling earrings that looked like coins strung together, and I never met a woman who could fix her hair in so many different shapes. We talked about many things, but mostly about men. She was dating a boy three years younger than she, and he kept telling her he didn't want to get married until he was "settled." *Mentiras*, the liar. She said, "You see how mature he is." She kept saying this like she was trying to convince me. *Pobrecita*, I thought, *you believe what the men tell you.*

✠ ✠ ✠

I sat up nights and embroidered anything I could get my hands on. I didn't embroider the pretty roses and curling leaves my mother taught me to embroider; I now had skeletons and dark-winged birds on my dish towels and bedsheets. I stitched and thought about why I had come here, why I was the one of my mother's seven daughters to follow her five sons across the border because I didn't want to stay behind and embroider table covers for the next wedding. I wanted more than dry, sleepy afternoons preparing tamales with *las señoras*. Making cheese. Watching *novelas*. I didn't want to be like the other girls in Ramblas, waiting for Christmas or Mother's Day or El Día de los Muertos, when the boys returned home for a visit puffed with pride and American dollars. I fixed my hair for them, decided for weeks what to wear

to the dances that would celebrate them after they had left me
with *los niños* and our suffering mothers, who longed for them.

I said to Carol, my American friend, "Have you ever had a
Mexican man?"

We sat on the steps leading to my apartment and watched
Mrs. Hidalgo's pantyhose swing on a clothesline.

"A Brazilian," she said, "but it wasn't all it's cracked up to be.
I don't know—I think he intimidated me. You know, all that stuff
you hear. I wasn't sure I was up to it."

Carol bit into an orange slice, and juice squirted from her
mouth. Her hair was held off her face by a tie-dyed scarf, and she
braided the rest into two big loops.

"Why?" she asked. "Are they worth it?"

"I don't know," I said. "I never slept with anyone before I
married my husband."

✘ ✘ ✘

In the mornings, I looked in my husband's sock drawer or closet
and counted the number of shirts and rolled knee-highs he had
left behind. I always woke up with renewed hope and thought
maybe Carol was right. I counted these things because I thought
he wouldn't have left so many behind. There were too many.

Sometimes I called my mother in Mexico. She was usually
watching a *novela* with my little sister. I didn't tell her my husband had left me. It was hard to keep her attention for very long.
She'd start to weep on the phone, and I'd say, "What happened,
Mamá?" and she'd say, "Oh, *m'ija*, the lady on the television looks
just like you."

Mi hija. My daughter. I called when I knew my father wasn't
home. I thought about the deal I'd made with my *papi* after his
last son finished school and left for the border. My father was
standing beneath a tree, *un pino triste*, with his low mustache, his

long gaze, and his cowboy hat lowered to cover the knot above his right eye. I knew I was his favorite daughter. I said, "Papi, let me finish school." None of his daughters had completed more than three grades. "I can still do my chores," I told him. "Pay for me to finish school."

He dug his boot into the dry earth, *la tierra de* Guanajuato, the state he never left in his entire life. But he was still the smartest man in Ramblas. He read books about Egypt and he knew how to handwrite, unlike my mother, who never had an education.

"Why do you want to return to school?" he asked, lowering his eyes on me. "So you can meet a man, marry, and quit? You want me to pay for that?"

"No, Papi," I said. "I won't marry in school, and I promise I'll graduate."

The wind whistled through the tree. My father saw a fisherman with a pole bent over the ledge of *la presa*, his thin shoulders hunched as if the small anchor pulled them. I said urgently, "Papi," and I almost grabbed his thick brown wrist. He would stop and talk to any stranger, my father, no matter what he was doing. On dusty back roads in the hills, or walking a dried riverbed, he would sense, like a dog smells a buried bone, a stranger to talk to. His eyes would look over the horizon, squinting in concentration, and never focus on the stranger's face. He would talk for hours about the harvest, the weather, the latest family to lose sons to the border, but mostly he would listen.

He turned and stepped onto the stone dam, making his way to the lone fisherman. I followed behind him in open-toed sandals, carefully picking my steps. I knew I had lost his attention, and I searched around me for something to fill the time I would spend waiting. But there was nothing and nobody. How often my brothers, sisters, and I wished he would meet strangers in town. If he met them in a crowded bus station or near the *zócalo*, we could occupy ourselves easily. But he never did. In those places he walked as the stranger, with a stone face and rigid posture; he would say he had to get back to the ranch by noon.

"*Buenos días*," my father said to the fisherman.

I found a smooth stone jutting out of the dam and took my seat ten feet from them. I picked up a gray rock and threw it at a bird searching for something to eat between the stones. Father stood with his hands clasped on his hips, his dusty black leather jacket open and rising above his stomach. They stared across the lake. I could hear them talking about *la bruja de Aguascalientes*. The fisherman said he had a deaf friend, and this witch, she made it so that he could hear again. Their voices droned on and blended with the wind until I wasn't aware of their talking and I daydreamed.

"Marta, *venga*," my father called to me. The fisherman looked in my direction. His eyes crinkled in a smile, but his mouth remained turned down.

I lifted myself from the stone and shuffled toward them.

"Marta," my father said, "I have asked Don Tomas what he thinks about your promise."

I stared at the fisherman, this stranger, with his empty fishnet and slack orange pole, and then looked back to my father with wide eyes.

"I told him about *tu promesa de quedarte soltera*, and he told me, '*Déjala*—let her go.'"

The fisherman looked down at his worn canvas shoes. "If you want it," he said to the wet stone beneath his feet.

⚒ ⚒ ⚒

Carol took me to a pet shop to buy me a bird. We picked out a green one with yellow cheeks; the man behind the counter showed us three different types of birdseed. I asked him, "Will it talk?"

"Not unless you give him vocal cords," he said, laughing.

To Carol I said under my breath, "Too bad—I would teach it to say *pendejo*."

Carol laughed out loud, and her earrings jangled. She liked it when I cursed in Spanish.

At home, I watched the bird eat its seed. I tried to see if it swallowed. This bird, I liked to watch him bathe. He would flutter into himself, burying his face in his feathers. And he had such courage, my bird. He flew headfirst into my windowpanes without a second thought. The next day, he would do the same thing. He sang clear and beautiful. It didn't matter that he was without vocal cords.

I thought about the fisherman with his pole and no fish. My father called him *un testigo*—the witness to my promise. I was the only daughter to complete a high school education and the only one to leave *la casa de mi padre soltera*. Unmarried.

I remember my father's face on the day of my graduation. He came home drunk after toasting my achievement in a *pulquería* full of strangers. He sat straight and glassy-eyed in a small cluster of waving parents. I remember thinking his strangers had been my helpers. If I hadn't had *un testigo*, would I have finished school? I watched Papi remove his hat, something he did only in churches and a few moments before laying his crop-weary body to bed. The lump above his brow shone brightly against the old adobe walls.

✂ ✂ ✂

"Carol," I said one afternoon, watching her pick the green peppers from her rice, "do you still think he'll come home?"

She looked up at me with a long face. She was sad and quiet on this day. Her young boyfriend had left her for a girl with straight teeth. I asked her this question to remind her that her problem was nothing.

She brought a pink fingernail to her temple and tapped it there. "You know," she said, "I didn't know how to say this to you, but I'm not so sure anymore."

She brought her legs up on the chair and wrapped her arms around her knees. I felt sad now, because I hadn't expected her to finally tell me the truth. I looked at the bird in his cage. I had tied bows of red ribbon on the bars, and the one he pecked rested loose on the floor. I watched him clean his feathers. His beak worked rapidly.

Carol said, "From now on, I may sleep with younger men, but I'll never picture them at the altar, Martha, I swear it."

⁂ ⁂ ⁂

In the morning, I walked to the water, and my steps made the wood dock creak. I read the names of the boats: *Treasure Chest*, *Whimsy*, *Dolores*. Who was Dolores? I passed two guys with skin like my own sitting with their legs dangling over the edge of the dock. One of them hissed—"*Chi, chi, chi*"—and I kept staring at the boats. I thought about Carol. I wondered about me. We needed *testigos*, she and I, a face off the street.

I passed an old woman with a paper sack, but she didn't see me. I remembered my father had bought three fish, but the fisherman had no change, so he kept the money and Papi chose two more. They were the only fish he caught all day. They were silver and yellow in the sunshine, and they flopped around the stone dam. I stood next to my father and watched the fisherman take a buck knife and slit their stomachs while they still sucked for breath. I watched the red life drain out of them.

The fisherman took them down to the water and rinsed them off. He brought them back glistening and smooth, and held them out to us like an offering. My father nudged me to take them, and then he said to the fisherman, "I think we will have rain tomorrow."

Pier at Dusk

After Robbe-Grillet

From a fishing bench on an old wood pier, a fisherman's back faces the sinking sun. He cracks a pumpkin seed in his mouth, eats the light green nut, and throws the shell into the cool, metallic ocean below. A second discarded shell follows, and then another, dropping lightly from the side of the pier in slow, rhythmic succession. The open bag of pumpkin seeds rests on the bench next to him. The waves beat the weathered supports with a swinging motion, giving the pier the appearance of a rocking hammock with an old man weighted in its center. His eyes hold the reflection of an elongated bay, its coastline beginning to twinkle.

He sits with his knees apart and baits a hook with a piece of cheese. It is the bait he has always used; he doesn't care what they sell at the new tackle shop at the end of the pier. The bright blue roof of the shop impedes his view of the islands. He would like to disassemble the shop plank by plank and restore the pier to its original shape. The cheese on the end of the hook is a neat cube cut by a precise knife.

The sun collapses on the horizon. Seagulls leave their posts. The fisherman sits and waits for the darkness to follow. He will drop his line into the ocean when the water becomes a shadow to the sky. The line will hang invisible, and he will hear the water break beneath him, see his pole rest on the hand-worn guardrail before him, and feel himself an isolated settler on his own island. He will wait for the tug from below and pull glints of silver toward him, forming a pile of shimmering loaves at his feet, one after another, from an ocean that never cheats him.

The fisherman removes the cotton from his ears. The cool air rushes to fill the void. He plugs his ears with cotton when coming down from the hill with his pole, crossing the overpass above the pulsating rush-hour traffic. The population has increased, and the man on the street asks for loose change. With a hand oiled and tanned from years of fishing, he reaches into the front pocket of his canvas coat for two clean balls of cotton. They are white; they are pure between his fingers. He pushes one into each ear, the cold air softens, the sounds muffle, his head is the smooth inside of a seashell.

The dog crosses the beach diagonally, leaving wet prints on the sand. The dog is a bronze color, short-haired, with skin taut around the outline of his ribs. He skims across the sand at the same even pace. His shoulders bounce; his flanks stretch and retract with the motion.

The small lead sinker on the fisherman's pole hangs close to the hook. It's the platinum color of the ocean at nightfall. It will take his line to a surface he will not be able to see in the darkness, a thin line to the space below.

The fisherman's hands rest on the fishing pole, bracing his weight. He sees and hears nothing beside him, his eyes reflecting pools of the tide stretching itself across the sand. The ocean gains strength as evening approaches. The rhythm melts a sandcastle, washes the shore clean. The waves beat beneath him.

Across the pier from the fisherman are three boys. He does not see or hear them; he does not know they are there. A second-hand fishing pole lies next to them, cast aside, awaiting its use. In a plastic bucket rest three bottles of soda pop, unopened. The boy with the light skin leans over the guardrail to watch a piece of cardboard drift by; it jerks forward and slides back with the motion of the current. The three boys face the last sliver of sun, unlike the fisherman, whose white-gray head reflects the pink cast of the sky.

The dark-skinned boy has no shoelaces in his shoes. The leather is hardened from afternoons spent wading in salt water while he preys on loose mussels and cracked sand dollars during low tide. He paces a small circle near the other two, his eyes fixed on his feet passing over the wood planks. He is careful to step over the spaces between the planks of the pier as if they were cracks in a sidewalk bringing ten years' bad luck. He circles and circles. The water churns beneath him. His steps create a rhythm on the pier, hollow notes the fisherman cannot hear. They reverberate but are so slight the fisherman feels them to be the pier breathing, the old wood.

The water grows more brilliant as the light fades. The ocean sparkles at its points of height, as if the crests of swells hold blinking lanterns. The third boy picks at a calcified rock with his pocketknife. He is trying to pry an embedded shell from its crevice. He works the knife fervently, locks of his sandy brown hair bouncing in his eyes. Periodically, he lifts his knife from the task to check the position of the sun. He can stare at the descending red arc, unlike in the hours before sunset, when a look at the sun brings white splotches to his vision. He returns to the pockmarked rock in his hand, the small white shell holding fast to its age-old anchor.

When the last seagull takes flight, its lost feathers float and then catch in the large cracks of the pier. Where the water does not reach, crystalline sand dims like smoldering ash, becomes cool, textured, and heavy. The dry wood of the pier grows solid with moisture. It appears to halt its sway, silence its creaks, and fortify itself against the strong night tide.

The fisherman sits very still in the last movement of light. His callused hands hold the fishing pole motionless. His eyes do not blink. He feels the pier contract and expand; the water at this precise moment swirls and spreads itself noiselessly across the beach; the pink wisps of cloud fade from the sky; the entire earth, it seems to him from his seat on the pier, holds its breath for the passing, the change to darkness. And then the fisherman is facing the moon. The sinker drops. The dog peers into a trash can, and the boys throw their bottle caps over the guardrail.

Joint Custody

I

Ann wheeled her smart Travelpro luggage to the edge of the curb and stepped onto Fifth Avenue, shooting her hand straight into the air. *Taxi!* her hand declared. But the streets were eerily quiet. Summertime in New York. The neighborhood, in its morning lavender glow, awakening after the rush of people had fled for the weekend in Hampton jitneys, overstuffed cars, or crowded trains. She still felt exhilarated when she hailed a cab. Like a maestro, someone in charge. S-O-M-E-O-N-E, as a matter of fact. It didn't matter that no cabs were around, dwindling from city streets by app-wielding millennials. "Taxi!"

She couldn't help noticing how light she felt. God, wasn't it terrible? Emily had been gone two days, and Ann wasn't falling apart or calling her every second to see how she was. She was actually looking forward to a summer in London, living in a colleague's flat like a college student studying abroad—something she had never had the opportunity to do but now could almost pretend to. Everything new and waiting to be explored. A new city, by herself, as if she were in a new life. But of course she wasn't; it only felt like that as she checked her watch and stretched her neck to see several blocks ahead for that one yellow cab floating down the avenue.

Margaret had called her with the update: Emily dropped off, Tom the same, with the exception of a school-age girlfriend. School-age? Well, college-age. Whatever. Too young for him, but, then again, what mature woman would be with Tom? They had laughed, but Ann remembered being that school-age girl enamored with philosophical Tom and his unconventional outlook on everything from deodorant to employment. Oh, the freedom of it! The romance. You and me against the world. A lifetime ago.

She hadn't wanted to call Emily right away and had agreed to phone her when she arrived in London. Give her time to settle in with her dad. Don't hover. She knew they would need the space and time to reacquaint, and she didn't want to be accused of interfering with that. And she was fine, really. The girlfriend was momentarily irritating—of course he would not have mentioned it to her before Emily arrived so Ann could prepare her. She wondered how Emily was dealing with it. Would she welcome another woman to talk to, or would she view it as an intrusion into her relationship with her father?

Instead of a cab, here was old Mr. Bastible, ambling down the sidewalk with his cart. There seemed to be one eccentric, busybody person in every apartment building in New York City, keeping abreast of the coming and goings of all the tenants, like some kind of genealogist. He took his squeaky red cart out every morning to the market and came back with what? Sometimes a paper towel roll, a few apples, cans of cat food for Persian Minerva. He liked to talk. A lot. Mostly about other people's lives or the baseball games he watched religiously. His favorite team the Mets, of course. Always wore his Mets cap over the tufts of gray-black

hair that formed a hedge along the sides of his head. Stout man
with a limp that seemed to propel the cart forward.

"Whaddaya doin' out so early on a Saturday mornin'? Goin'
somewhere?"

"Yes, Mr. Bastible. I'm going to London. But I can't seem to
catch a cab."

"Ya gotta hold ya hand higha. Like this." He waved so fero-
ciously that he almost fell over.

"Careful, Mr. Bastible."

"You gotta man out there? That'd be nice for your little girl."

"No, no. I'm going for work." What she really meant was,
*Well, there's one man I'm interested in, though I've told nobody, not
even Margaret,* yet the sound of his voice over the phone, even
through his emails, created a little spark, like a jolt of caffeine,
her heart pumping a little faster, her mind fully alert. But what
was the point, really? She had never met Douglas in person. They
had begun working together on the picture book for wider pub-
lication only in the past quarter. Originally a French children's
book. *On the High Seas.* A little boy in a French sailor outfit takes
his rowboat out on the water for a delicious ride that carries him
to many enchanting villages along the coast. He explores the
culture of each—*pétanque* in the village square with the locals, for
instance—in a kind of picture travel book. A boy on an adventure,
à la Maurice Sendak, but without the goblins. They were working
on the series idea: *On the High Seas: England; On the High Seas:
America.* They had discussed the little boy eating lobster on the
Cape, picking blueberries in Maine. Then the publisher decided:
We really must bring you two together. Work with the author,
who can come up to London.

Mr. Bastible nodded. He knew she was lying. No one got that
dressed up to fly anymore. She had on a crisp pleated skirt that
rested just above her knees, in a way that women who have good

legs can pull off. And she did, he noticed. It would be a waste for them not to be greeted by a starched shirt on the other side of the Atlantic. *Give this girl a break*, he thought. For years he had watched her coming and going with the little girl, hauling groceries, taking her to school, arriving in a rush from work with a heavy satchel weighing down her shoulder. "Hello, Mr. Bastible; Good morning, Mr. Bastible," she always said when she passed him on the streets or coming through the doorway of their building, in a rush, always in a rush, usually pulling her little girl's hand along with her.

Not for nothing, but it broke his heart. He was an old man with no family, and they had become his family. His apartment-building family. Folks he could count on to know him, to spot him, to say, "Hey, we haven't seen Mr. Bastible for a while." And that was worth a lot to him. Just enough. Because he wouldn't really want to move in with them. Just enough to consider them family. Though they wouldn't know it. He wouldn't want them to know it, because, well, it was maybe a little pathetic. Letting people know you were lonely in New York City was pathetic. Especially to these young folk, who were busier than he'd ever known folks to be, running here and there, holding down jobs that seemed to demand more out of them. Checking their phones, i-whatevers, and staring at their laptop screens in the coffee shops like they were reading about something as important as the world coming to an end.

People like Ann were too busy to be lonely, he thought. Today they could skip the marriage part altogether and jump straight to the end. Not like in his day, when having sex with a woman meant you were marrying her, having kids, paying a mortgage, working at the same company like a good soldier until you received the gold watch and a pension.

Mr. Bastible had missed that part. The part with the gold watch and the pension. Well, to be honest, the part with marriage and kids too. But almost. It had been going in that direction. He'd

worked for Jeanne's father in the family deli. He was quick with
the sandwiches. Lunch rush was a challenge to him, and he rose
to it. Turkey, lettuce, tomato, Swiss with mayo on a toasted roll in
two minutes flat. I kid you not. Two minutes. He held the record
in the deli, but Jeanne's older brother didn't like it. He was jealous
of Mr. Bastible and didn't like the attention he was getting from
Papa, what with Papa getting older, Mr. Bastible set to marry his
sister, and the deli's future hanging in the balance.

"You know how to run a business," old Papa had said to him.
He was good with numbers too, and had a few ideas about why
the deli was running a deficit. Jeanne's brother had watched out
of the corner of his eye. Things got rough. Jeanne's brother made
it rough, and Mr. Bastible wasn't known for his tolerance of nonsense. One day it came to fists in the storeroom. And guess who
ended up on the floor? Not I, said the fly! But wouldn't you know
it—Jeanne and Papa stood up for old brother boy, blood being
thicker than water with these people. So he was outta there. Take
your corned beef and shove it. Find another patsy for your single
daughter, someone who can tolerate nonsense up the wazoo.

So he'd spent the rest of his working life hopping around
delis. First in Brooklyn, then in Manhattan, where he was lucky
enough to find this rent-controlled apartment that was still his,
screw the developers always sniffing at his heels, and with social
security and the little savings he kept, he was okay, not high on
the hog, but just enough. Just enough.

But for Ann, he wanted more, watching her life as if she were
the daughter he never had. A good, hardworking man who would
take some of the load off, keep them safe, because didn't she know
there were wolves at the door?

"How long you gone for?"

Old Mr. Bastible, Anne thought, always into the business of
others. Nothing better to do with his time. Sad, really. Did he

have any family? She never saw a single person visit him. Just him and the cat. She'd thought about inviting him over for a meal once or twice, seeing what he was doing on Thanksgiving, but then it felt strange and the thought passed, a good intention dissolving away like a slip of fog.

"Most of the summer. I'll be working over there."

"You be speaking English by then," he joked. Anne laughed. He really could be funny. Every now and then the humor of old New Yorkers delighted her—an unexpected remark, witty and dry, to let you know the clock was still ticking, the brain still quick and sharp. Why hadn't she invited Mr. Bastible over before? It seemed so uncharitable now, so careless and self-involved.

Her life had been, she realized, one long push to survive since her divorce from Tom. She'd moved back to New York and began clawing her way to a job that would pay enough to keep her and Emily afloat. Not living with her parents or moving someplace where the rents were low and she pieced together jobs with masking tape. And she did it, really, with her laser-like focus on work, Emily, food, bills, doctors, school. Nothing else. The occasional night out with some girlfriends when Emily was old enough to go to sleepovers, but even then her mind was on all the things she wasn't doing when Emily was away: laundry, old lightbulb, cluttered closet, camp forms . . . It never ended.

And then, suddenly, there it was: a yellow taxi cab swooping around the corner like a powerboat coming to rest abruptly at a dock. It rocked back with the brakes, coming to a bouncy stop at her feet. Voilà! Old Mr. Bastible stepped back with his cart. Seeing him there with his puffy morning eyes, his old-man sneakers and socks, and the way his cloudy, dark eyes checked the man driving the cab, she felt like a teenage girl again, saying goodbye to her father at the entrance to her dorm room. She felt her heart swell with affection and felt the pull not to part, to linger in that feeling of protection, in that time when she was unconsciously free and safe.

"Bye, Mr. Bastible," she said, signaling the cabbie to open the trunk so she could swing her suitcase into it.

And just as Mr. Bastible took his hands off his cart automatically, his body moving to help her, Ann lifted the suitcase and heaved it into the cavernous trunk. One-two-three. Just like that. *The women today,* he thought, once again surprised, *expecting nothing and doing everything on their own while this jerk cabbie sits in the front seat, picking his nose.* "You'll miss the fireworks display this Fourth," he wanted to say, when the whole building, it seemed, climbed the stairs to the rooftop to watch it, a mass of humanity gathered together and the familiar warmth he felt when he saw her face, Emily's, with maybe one or two of her friends, and Ann staring at the evening sky for that burst of color and spectacle when they all mouthed, "Aw!" in unison and glanced at each other to see if they'd caught that special one.

"See you later," he said, barely looking at her and pushing his cart away with a heaving step.

"Goodbye!" she said to his back, feeling a little disappointed that he had turned away so soon.

Ann slid into the seat, careful not to sit on her skirt and wrinkle it, and snapped with authority, "JFK airport, please." In an instant, the driver switched on his blinker and dove to the corner to make the turn toward the East River. Through her window, she watched old Mr. Bastible pushing his cart up the sidewalk. She was leaving for the whole summer. She could hardly believe it.

II

The closer they came to El Roblar Drive, the less they talked, eyes riveted on the road before them, dust in swirls clouding the rearview mirror. The Toyota bounded over the dirt, the loose muffler clanging against the car's underbelly.

Margaret hated to be the one to drive Emily to her dad's for the summer, but she was Ann's best friend and couldn't let her down. She eyed Emily, seated next to her. Her long, light hair was held back in a ponytail, revealing the three silver studs in her left earlobe. She wore thick black boots with flare-legged jeans. A girl like Emily would be bored to tears in this sleepy outpost for the summer. Margaret felt some guilt for not having offered to keep Emily herself in Los Angeles, but the truth was, she had no idea what to do with a fourteen-year-old girl and couldn't imagine sharing her apartment for two months. And Margaret had a new boyfriend after a long, fallow period. *Still*, she thought.

"You've got the phone numbers?" Margaret asked.

"Yes."

"Maybe it would have been fun," Margaret thought out loud, "if you could have stayed with me."

Emily snickered, and Margaret couldn't tell if she thought it would be fun or not. But Emily only laughed about the length of time she overheard Margaret and her mother fretting over the phone about summer plans, even though they had more or less been settled since last spring. Her mother had the opportunity to work in the London office for the summer, so, after much deliberation, it was decided that Emily would fly to Los Angeles, where Margaret would pick her up and drive her to her father's town.

Emily suspected the indecision had more to do with her father than with her father's remote place. It was no secret that most people, including Margaret, thought her mother was better off without him. Yet Emily had never understood why, the secret of her parents' divorce known by everyone but her. Emily remembered only the fun times she had with her father, exploring nature and sharing books. It had been three years since she'd seen him, and her young memory of his life consisted mainly of the sights, smells, and feelings of his surroundings rather than his character. She had a dim mental outline of the cottage and the places on the grounds where she once liked to hike. There was the far irrigation ditch, where her fingers searched the soil for pieces of broken shell that her father said belonged to an earlier geological phase. And the place behind the cottage where a rope hammock stretched between two softly scented eucalyptus trees. The last time she visited, she had spent a few afternoons swinging in the hammock with her father, soothed by the rocking motion and the sound of his voice reading from *The Odyssey*.

They passed rows and rows of orange trees. Emily could see nothing beyond them, heavy globes and draping foliage filling the spaces between the trunks. The view out her window stood in stark contrast with her life in Manhattan, where she and her mother had moved a little more than three years earlier. She'd spoken to her dad a handful of times since then, mostly awkward holiday and birthday calls where all the time that had elapsed in between made the conversations seem forced. He rarely said much about his own life. As each year passed and Emily's and her mom's lives grew more full, she had a vague sense that maybe her father's life just stood still, the way it seemed to during her early childhood, and this thought was comforting from three thousand miles away.

The Toyota hit a bump in the road, and Emily's suitcase fell over in the back seat. She twisted around to right it. Through the dust rising toward the back window, she saw Mexican laborers with scarves tied around their mouths quickly pick the fat orange globes and then, just as fast, disappear behind the leaves.

Margaret missed all of this. Her eyes stayed fixed on the road, as if she refused to be taken in by the surroundings, seduced like Emily's father into a bucolic, nonproductive existence. Her smart cream-colored suit was at odds with the dust and aroma of manure that hung in the air. She had rolled the windows up tight the minute they left the freeway.

"How much farther?"

"I think it's just around the bend," Emily said.

"You think you'll recognize it?"

"I think so."

As they rounded the bend, Emily spotted the pale adobe cottage resting amid rows of young orange trees.

"Turn left at the blue mailbox," she said.

The Toyota slowed before the crooked box, which loomed larger through the front window. Margaret approached tentatively, the drive almost hidden beneath an overgrowth of weeds. She had never thought Tom would stay here as long as he had. She and Ann had often wondered when he would tire of this lifestyle and grow up, but he never did, and Margaret thanked the stars that her best friend knew when to get away.

Goriot, his old German shepherd, trotted slowly toward the moving car, his graying muzzle held up in a wrinkled bark. Emily rolled down the window and stuck her head out.

"Ruff-ruff," she barked back at him. The sight of the old dog and the crooked mailbox sent a swell of warmth and reassurance through her. Emily was surprised that she had forgotten these things, but here they were again, slightly aged but the same, waiting for her. Welcoming her.

From behind the cottage, Emily's father emerged. She stopped barking at Goriot. Her father was tanned, and his sandy gray hair was just long enough to be combed behind his ears. He had the same taut oval face and quick green eyes. His legs were still long and lean beneath his loose jeans, and if not for a little less hair in front and his slower gait, he would seem to have escaped time since Emily had seen him last.

"Welcome to my abode," he boomed, bowing with one hand at his waist, the other sweeping dramatically toward the weathered cottage. He did it to annoy Margaret, and secretly Emily smiled. He had an irreverent way. He used it on practically everyone in his life. When his last boss fired him, he told Emily over the phone, he'd asked her out on a date. "No more office conflict," he'd said with a chuckle.

Goriot loped around the car to greet Emily. She slid out and ruffled the fur on his head. "Well, Emily," her father said, "you're fortunate to have had this beautiful lady drive you here."

Leaning against the car, Margaret scanned him from head to toe, then fell blank at his face. "Haven't changed much, have you, Tom?"

Emily pulled her suitcase from the back seat and set it down on the ground so she could wrestle with Goriot, who clasped her arm lightly in his mouth, then tried to shake it like a loose rag. Emily felt more comfortable staring down at the dog than looking at her father. She wished she had come on her own, without Margaret to add to the tension.

"And you, Margaret," Tom said, "still fresh as daisies."

"Invite me in for something to drink, Tom. I'd like to see Emily settled."

Tom didn't respond. Instead he approached Emily in his well-worn moccasins. He'd missed her, and yet he didn't know how to say that. He felt the slight gnaw of guilt in his chest that he hadn't gotten on a plane sooner to see her. Time only passed. He held his arms out for a hug. He was surprised to find that the side of her face no longer pressed into the soft triangle of his stomach; she hit the bone-hard sternum of his chest. Did it make her feel like a stranger? he wondered. He wanted to hold her there for a long, deep minute, so that the time and distance might be erased. Emily stepped back.

"You're a young lady," Tom said. He quickly admired her before it made her feel uncomfortable. Then he reached for her suitcase.

"You look the same," Emily said.

"That's just what I wanted you to say." He laughed, putting Emily immediately at ease. She glanced at Margaret, whose expression hadn't changed, and she wished Margaret wouldn't follow them inside. "Now, let's get rid of her," Tom whispered to Emily, reading her mind, as they walked to the front door. The tiles on the patio were cracked, and the broken pieces tilted beneath their shoes. The patio was cool and shaded by the thick oak tree that slouched toward the cottage. Cacti were planted in a row of discarded ceramic pots, all of them chipped or split.

Tom opened the front door and stepped aside, mimicking a fancy doorman. Stepping in, Emily remembered how fascinating this little cottage had been to her when she was a girl. Tucked within the orange orchard, it had seemed like a place out of a fairy tale. Now, as she looked around, it seemed terribly confining. One large room was lined with books resting on shelves her father had made out of sagging plywood or old milk crates. It smelled musty and damp, the scent emanating from the yellowed pages of his used-book collection. The plaid futon he slept on was folded into the couch. A box holding an inflatable mattress rested in the center of the room. To the right, a small kitchen was separated from the room by a Guatemalan rug that hung from the ceiling. A square table, two chairs, and a rice-paper lamp were new additions to his home. Emily noticed a pair of women's sandals beneath the table and a peach sweater hanging from a hook on the wall.

"Well, how's New York?" Tom asked.

"It's all right." At that moment, Emily suddenly remembered that they'd be sleeping in the same room. She was too old to sleep on the futon with him now, and she glanced again at the inflatable mattress with a degree of relief.

"Your mother sounds busy. Traveling halfway around the world."

"Maybe halfway from here," Emily said, "but it's not so far from New York. It's a great opportunity for her."

"Opportunity," Tom said, grinning at her. He could hear her mother's voice in the way she said the word. "I suppose it is if you're interested in that sort of thing."

Emily sensed that she had to defend her mom. She had learned to read their undercover barbs like braille, the real words unseen but felt. Her mom liked her job at the publishing company, where they put out children's books with large, happy colored photographs. Emily liked watching her mom succeed, even though it meant being separated for the summer.

"She's working hard," Emily said. "And she's good at what she does." Then Emily thought she shouldn't have said that. Her dad might think she meant he didn't work hard enough. "How's the orchard?" she asked, quickly changing the subject.

"Just fine," he said. "A good crop this year. Evans plans to buy another acre in Matilija this fall."

Mr. Evans owned the cottage and the orchard surrounding it. He was an old farmer who wore a straw hat and elastic suspenders. When Emily saw him for the first time, she nearly laughed out loud. He gave the cottage to Tom at no charge for rent. In exchange, Tom kept watch over the grounds and helped manage the workers. When he wasn't doing that, he practiced mindfulness at the Happy Valley Foundation, run for thirty years by an Indian guru.

Margaret walked over to the table, where a tall glass was filled with purple wildflowers. Resting against the glass was an index card that read, "Welcome, Emily!" in bright red, female script, clearly not Tom's. Margaret picked up the card.

"Vicki wrote that," Tom said, walking behind the rug. "I think you'll like her, Emily. We met at the movie theater in town."

Margaret handed Emily the card. She stared down at it intently. "She's your girlfriend?" Emily asked.

"Did she sell you the popcorn?" Margaret chimed in.

The refrigerator door slammed shut. Tom took a deep breath behind the Guatemalan rug. He wished Emily had taken a bus from the airport, but he knew her mother had sent Margaret as a kind of emissary, to survey the environment for undesirable things, a new girlfriend probably one of them. In London, Ann was expecting a report. Margaret would sit down the first chance she got and dial her up so they could commiserate about his lifestyle. Nothing had changed. He wished Margaret long, unhappy karma.

"She lives here with me on the weekends. During the week she's a student at UCLA."

"She lives here with you?" Margaret wheeled around the table and headed for the rug. "Wait a minute, Tom. Did you tell Ann about this?"

"She knows I have a girlfriend." Tom came out from behind the rug with three glasses of water and a bowl of corn chips balanced on top.

"But the part about her living with you?"

"It's only two nights a week. She's taking summer-school courses, and in August she's going to Mexico with a group." Tom felt a twinge of guilt, but Ann would always find a reason to keep Emily to herself. He never would have had Emily for the whole summer if he had told Ann the entire story.

At that moment, a young woman walked through the door. She was wearing a royal-blue-and-white running outfit, her reddish hair pulled back in a ponytail. She had a broad, ruddy face and a look of practiced serenity. In her hand was a big, round orange, and when she saw them standing in the cottage, she brought her other hand to it and moved it in circles between her palms. To Margaret, she was shamelessly close to Emily's age. Emily thought she wasn't as pretty as her mother.

"Vicki," Tom called out, with a good amount of relief in his voice, "this is my daughter, Emily. Emily, this is Vicki."

Vicki moved forward too quickly, and the orange fell to the floor with a thud. She giggled, then kicked it out of her path. She wrapped both arms around Emily and said, "I'm glad you made it. I'm really looking forward to spending time with you this summer. Your dad's told me a lot about you."

Emily felt strangely frightened of Vicki, frightened of the churned-up feelings she was experiencing. Why hadn't anyone told her about a girlfriend? She wanted to push Vicki away out of anger or burst into tears, she wasn't sure which, so she looked to Margaret for some kind of help. But Margaret's eyes were fixed on Tom. She heard Margaret ask, "When does she graduate from college?"

Vicki stepped back, sensing she had moved too fast but not sure how to correct it. She wanted Emily to like her, and, more important, she wanted Tom to see that Emily liked her too. He was the first real grown man she'd been with. Vicki marveled at the way he chose to live. He didn't even own a car. He was like a pure, modern-day philosopher, eschewing all desire for material goods and capitalist striving. Some days she wondered if she could be that austere and uncomplicated. When she told her friends about him, they were impressed, and when they met him, they were a little awed.

"I'm not sure I'll be here all summer," Emily mumbled.

"Oh?"

"Hi, I'm Margaret. Emily's mother's friend." Margaret left Tom and stood, now, between Emily and Vicki.

"Hi. Did you hit a lot of traffic from the airport?"

"No. Smooth sailing. Do your parents live around here?"

"In the next town," Vicki said. Then, sensing that something was being evaluated, she added, "They really like Tom."

"I almost dated her mother," Tom broke in, "but she thought I was too old."

Vicki laughed. She looked adoringly at Tom. Margaret knew immediately that for as long as Tom kept some of his looks, this would be the kind of woman he could date—young and idealistic. She made a mental note to tell this to Ann.

Emily began to examine the room as if she'd never been there before. For the first time, she didn't find her dad's joke funny. Vicki had laughed alone.

"You're going to Mexico this August?" Margaret asked.

"With a preservation group. One of my professors is the head of a team working to preserve the ruins in Chichén Itzá."

"Oh," Margaret said. "Maybe this professor will work on Tom next."

At this everyone laughed, except for Emily, who reached into her jacket pocket to feel for the scrap of paper with her mother's London number on it.

"Well," Margaret said to Tom, reaching for her bag, "if you told Ann all of this and she's okay with it . . . ."

"Always nice to see a friend of Ann's," Tom said, standing by the door he'd opened for her. Emily did not think her mother knew the girlfriend would be living with them. She would have told her, wouldn't she? Part of her wanted to shout this, but a larger part didn't want to get her dad in trouble. She hated him for putting her in this position.

Margaret hugged Emily. "You're sure you've got the numbers?"

Emily nodded, her fingers still touching the slip of paper in her pocket, as if it were her lifeline. Her mother's number, and

Margaret's in LA. Margaret gave her a kiss on the cheek. Emily watched her move out of the cottage, leaving her with her dad and Vicki, and she wanted to run after her, but she couldn't behave as if she were a little girl.

"You know," Margaret whispered to Tom as she passed him, "you could mail those checks to Ann once in a while." She knew this would change nothing, but she couldn't let him forget the years Ann had struggled. Tom wondered why Margaret believed it her place to scold him. Emily caught the comment and understood what it meant, though she had never understood those comments before. She looked at her dad to see his reaction.

"Don't keep LA waiting," he said, closing the door behind her.

When Emily heard Margaret's Toyota leaving the drive, she walked over to the milk crate in which Tom continued to store books he wanted Emily to read. Attached to the crate was another index card in Vicki's hand, which read, "Emily's Book Box." She pulled the top book from the crate. On the cover was a paddleboat with a tattered gray flag sticking out of it. *Heart of Darkness*.

"You're going to love that," Tom said, walking back to the kitchen for something more to drink. Emily put the book back in the crate and sat down on the chair next to Vicki.

"I've already read it," she said. She suddenly hated the new book he'd picked for her, hated even more the idea that he didn't know she'd read it. Even her carefully tagged milk crate seemed a reminder of a useless, worn-out tradition. The cottage no longer held the same fairy-tale fascination for her. It seemed now like an old hippie den for a man who refused to grow up. She fought the urge to call her mother right then and tell her it was unfair to leave her with the man she'd left.

She stood up. "I'm going to take Goriot for a walk."

"Are you all right?" Tom walked out of the kitchen.

"I'm fine," she said, heading for the door.

"Supper on the porch tonight. Vicki's made some wonderful tabbouleh," he said, knowing that he sounded lamely upbeat. "We've had spectacular sunsets this week."

Emily kept walking. She remembered how he treated sunsets, rainstorms, any slight change in the typical weather forecast as if he were experiencing it for the first time. Again and again. At one time, Emily had thought this was the greatest thing about him.

She left Goriot at the end of the drive. Goriot sat at its edge, too old now to risk stepping over the line that separated his home from the rest of the world. She looked back at the dog twice, his head lowered, watching her decrease in size. She walked faster. Then, when she thought no one was looking, she broke into a run.

Tom realized how much time had passed when Goriot no longer followed her. She had eyes like her mother's, deep hazel, then a light yellow and green in certain light. The similarity had startled him at first, the child's wide, sparkling innocence gone and replaced by her mother's unmistakable gaze.

Emily vanished. Christ, he thought, the kid was smart. She had known better than he that they would not be picking up where they'd left off three years before. And Margaret had been no help, surveying the cottage like a jail warden.

Had he been too cavalier about Vicki? Something told him he had been, and he wished he'd answered Emily more openly. Of course Vicki was his girlfriend. Why had he said that she only spent weekends with him, like some kind of boarder? His tongue had grown thick with stupidity and defensiveness.

He turned the corner at El Roblar, leaving tracks in the dust where Emily's steps had fallen. He was following her, but he had no idea what he would say when he caught up. Ann had come home one night, gone out on the balcony of the small apartment they'd rented in Silver Lake, and told him the marriage was over. That was the truth, no matter how many times he'd reshaped it into a symmetrical form of mutual consent in his mind. Nobody had ever explained the divorce to Emily. Maybe that had been a mistake.

Tom caught a glimpse of Emily's blue jacket swinging around the fourth block. El Roblar had been the original main street, abandoned for a fancier commercial row in the town next door. Since then, the street shops were occupied by a rotating series of artisans, secondhand traders, and small-appliance fix-it specialists. In a good year, the storefronts wove together in a pattern of broken vacuum cleaners, leather saddles, carved wooden eagles, oil paintings, glass jam jars, and old radios. The fix-it specialists survived the longest. The others stayed for a year, perhaps two if they were lucky.

He had taken Emily to Bill's Trading Post when she was a little girl. She liked to sit in the old saddle resting on a sawhorse beside the window, her feet just reaching the stirrups. They had looked through '60s music albums with faded and worn covers, his knowledge of each band thrilling her.

⌘ ⌘ ⌘

Emily headed for the Ventura River, where she felt like chucking some rocks into the charging water. She cut through the Demses' property, stopping at the chain-link fence around Howard Dems's house. Dems was a retired geologist who had turned his yard into a sanctuary for injured tortoises. He took them in from zoos, deserts, foreign lands, and nursed them back to health. Emily remembered that he had once had a tortoise from Kenya, a great big one with a bad crack in its shell. Dems had said the crack would take years to heal. Its armor-like shell would grow more slowly than was measurable by the human eye, and there was something in that fact that gave Emily comfort now.

She stopped to grip the fence with both hands and searched the yard. The tortoises were harder to spot, since Dems had planted more shrubs along the fence. She ducked her head to look below a bush. It was then that she spotted her father out of the corner of her eye. He hung back, and his hesitancy made her feel angry. What was he waiting for?

Judy Dems walked toward her from the center of the yard, where a large garden umbrella stood. Most days, she sat under it with a tall glass of iced tea and kept watch over the tortoises. She looked exactly like her husband—stout build, square face, and glasses—except for the khaki-colored hat she wore to protect her face from the sun. She came around the shrubs. "Emily Norris!" Judy said. "Tom's daughter?"

Emily released the fence and stepped back, surprised to be recognized. Tom stopped at a tree and watched the scene from afar, feeling pleasure in the fact that Emily was experiencing some personal history in his world.

"How you've grown," Judy said, bringing a hand to her mouth.

"Does Mr. Dems still fish?" she asked.

"Oh, no," Judy said. "The river's all dried up. Rocks and stone now."

"Really? All of it?"

"Not a drop."

They talked about the drought and the health of a few tortoises, and then Emily left quickly, promising to stop by again. Her arms pumped hard with the rhythm of her long stride, and she got some pleasure out of leaving the scene so fast and wondering if her father would follow her now. She felt in control for the first time in her life. She *could*, she wanted to scream, make decisions on her own.

Tom felt as if he were missing a piece of the teenage puzzle he might never have the chance to find. He wanted to talk to her about their bumpy start, but it seemed like a high wall he'd need practice climbing over. She seemed to require a new language that he hadn't had the chance to gather.

The drought had wrung the river into a dry bed of chalk-white stones and rusted cans. From the edge of the embankment, Tom watched Emily pick across the jagged points and loose rocks, not choosing her steps carefully yet bounding over them easily.

He stopped following her. He stood and watched as she grew smaller. He suspected she knew he was there but chose to ignore him. She stopped at the point where the cypress grew and hoisted herself up the other side of the embankment by its exposed root.

A horse stable sat on the other side. At least a dozen horses stood in pipe corrals three yards back from the river. Tom had a friend who kept a horse there, a retired park ranger. He had taken Emily to the stable when she was younger, and she'd been startled by the little kicks and quick tail swats the horses used to keep flies off. She'd been frightened of the horses at first but then had quickly come to love them, as he had known she would. He had known how to read Emily in those years.

Emily knew he wouldn't come over the riverbed, given the more careful way he walked now. But she knew he was still there, watching, wondering where she was going, what she would do next, she wanted to shock him. The horses were eating their afternoon hay, their teeth grinding in the hollow of their aluminum feed bins. Occasionally one of the bins lifted and hit the fence, creating a booming, metallic sound.

Emily stopped at the last corral and struggled to unhook the latch. She grabbed the bridle hanging from a hook on the stall. She glanced quickly at the riverbed, and Tom knew she saw him. She backed a bay-colored horse away from its feeder and then expertly slid the bit into its cavernous mouth. The horse reached impatiently for its food. Emily stumbled but kept hold of the reins.

Tom couldn't believe she really meant to ride. What was she doing? Parental worry returned like a familiar, anxious friend. Did she know how dangerous this was? He was caught between his surprise that she was now brave enough to do this and panic that she might follow through on her plan. *You can't take that horse out!* he wanted to shout. *It's not even yours!*

"Put him back!" Tom yelled from across the riverbed. When she was four, she'd almost taken a shiny compass from a store. He'd waited to see if she would actually slip it into her pocket, as he'd watched her eyes covet it for ten long minutes while she struggled with the knowledge that she might not get away with it.

Emily's leg swung over the horse's bare back, her eyes never lifting from its dark mane. Tom cleared his throat to shout again, but he knew she would refuse to hear him. The horse lunged toward the thin trail that lined the river's edge.

"Emily!" he shouted.

But Emily squeezed the horse's rib cage so that loose pebbles spun from its hard hooves as they dashed away. She passed through the hard summer shadows while Tom tried to scramble across the riverbed. Who is she? he wondered, with a little panic. No longer daddy's little girl. Emily looked back once, felt a guilty sense of satisfaction, then rode away.

Grace

All summers in California were traumatic.

At the close of each school year, the sun grew hot, daylight seeped into evening, and every flaw and imperfection of my life with my mother, Grace, became glaringly bright.

I never thought of a California summer the way the rest of the world did: bikinis, suntanned bodies, and Hollywood movie stars. I lived the story behind the glossy stage, where old costumes and scaffolding and wires hung loose and exposed.

I lived in Milapas, near the glittering coast, but the coast where immigrants fished, fat families swam, and allergy-ridden souls sought an afternoon of salt air and sunshine. I was one of the allergy-ridden, my nose and eyes a scratchy red during ragweed season. But Grace never had time to take me to the shore. She was a single mom in the 1970s. Divorce ran rampant in California, so why should I have thought that summer would be any different from the rest?

My mother's name was Grace Mulroy and then, after the divorce, Grace Caple. I've called her Grace ever since I can remember. She called me J.D., which is short for Jonathan Daniel.

If I try to remember what went wrong with Grace that summer, I always come back to the divorce. Even though my dad had left her three years before, I realize now that maybe there are some things people can never forget—maybe they just keep living the same old story.

For a while, though, our lives seemed to move on. After the divorce, Grace went to a police auction and bought herself a Dodge. It was older and longer than most cars and had large chrome bumpers, fishtails, and orange paint as bright as the hair of a clown. We drove the Dodge everywhere, up and down the coast, over rolling hills to the inland valleys, the wind rushing through our open windows and our arms outstretched to catch it.

Grace loved that Dodge. It seemed to remind her of freedom, when she was anything but free. She called it her dinosaur, and she would say to me, "J.D., pack yourself in the 'saur. We're going somewhere."

I soon learned that "somewhere" could mean many things to Grace. It could mean a trip to the grocery store for a half pint of milk or a change in our home address.

What I could depend on was a trip to the bookstore during my first week of summer. Grace would take me there as a reward for getting through another year of school. It was no different that summer. We drove down Highway 33 toward Ojai, passed the lone billboard on that stretch. The bookstore was fifteen miles from Al's apartment in Ventura. Al was Grace's boyfriend, and we'd been living with him since last Christmas.

The bookstore was outdoors. Twisted branches of an old oak tree spread blocks of shade across the bookstalls. I looked for books about creatures outside of my time. I could spend hours scouring the three booths of children's books for the one that escaped me, the one with the purple dragon sliding awkwardly across a linoleum kitchen floor. These creatures used to live inside my books, and outside them too. I could call them up whenever I wanted, transform a porch column into a brontosaurus's leg, transport myself to somewhere else, someplace rich, green, and lush.

Grace left her sandals in the Dodge. She liked to walk barefoot. When we walked through the front gate of the bookstore, I could hear her feet slapping against the concrete floor. "Hi, Tom," she said to the man behind the counter. Tom had a white handlebar mustache growing around his mouth and a low belly that hung over the rim of his pants. He wore jeans with a set of keys hanging from the belt loop, a black leather jacket, and boots that completed his motorcycle outfit. He knew the location of every book in that store and would stroke his long mustache while thinking about the best way to direct you to it.

"How've you been?" Grace asked.

"Staying alive," he said.

I ran to the children's booth, tore through a stack of books sitting on the first shelf. Grace came up behind me and rested a hand on my head. "Take it easy, J.D.," she said. "You going to put the books back where you found them?"

I broke free of her hand, tore through another stack. Grace sat down on the bench and lit a cigarette. She used to sit next to me on that bench and read me a book. Sometimes she would buy the book and finish reading it to me at bedtime. We would lie on the bed, our toes stretched before us, and the sound of the book opening reminded me of my shoe coming down on a mound of brittle leaves. I loved the sound.

But then things changed. Grace got a job waiting tables at night. She told Carol, her best friend, that she didn't want me to have a welfare mom. She'd come home smelling like the leftover fish kebabs she'd bring me from the restaurant. I grew sick of fish kebabs. If Grace got off early, she'd come sit next to me on the bed in her uniform, smelling of fish, fish, fish. I told her I was too old for bedtime stories.

Grace looked at the other people in the bookstore and blew smoke out the side of her mouth. She propped a leg on top of her knee and bounced her bare foot, as if she were keeping time with the Bonnie Raitt songs she listened to. She had no interest in books. She used the time, it seemed to me, to go someplace far away in her mind, so far that if I said her name, she'd jump as if I'd slapped her.

"When you're through, J.D., come here. I need to tell you something."

I couldn't find the dragon book. I took my time looking for it, because the tone in Grace's voice made me think I didn't want to hear what she had to say. I pulled a book called *Sea Mammals* from a stack. On the cover was a picture of a giant whale next to a man in a green tie. The man was there to show how big the whale was. Stupid. A fish or mermaid would have made better sense. A man couldn't stand next to a whale underwater with a tie on, and a whale couldn't stand next to a man on the beach. The book said it was a blue whale. It looked gray to me.

Grace put out her cigarette when I sat next to her. A bad sign. It meant she was getting ready to leave. She crushed it into the seat of the bench, brushed the butt and ashes into the square of dirt around the oak tree. She hadn't put cucumbers on her eyes that morning. They were puffy and small. Grace's best friend, Carol, had read about cucumbers in a beauty magazine. The magazine said cucumbers would take years from eyes slouched saggy after a rough night. When we stayed at Carol's after my father left, she and Grace would lie on the floor with slices of cucumbers balanced on their lids while I fed them chocolate Grahamy Bears until the box was empty.

"J.D.," Grace said, putting her arm around me. It made me uncomfortable. I squirmed until she lifted her arm and set it above me on the backrest. "Hon, we're moving back to Mrs. Clark's for a while. It's not working out with Al."

Mrs. Clark was the old lady we lived with before Al. In between John, Grace's old boyfriend, and Al. She was the manager of the fish restaurant my mother worked at, and she wore the same square-collared, puffy-sleeved uniform she made on her sewing machine in sets of a dozen.

"Are you going to quit smoking?" I flipped through *Sea Mammals* to make sure it was the book I wanted. I knew Grace would buy me a book today.

"I don't know, J.D. Did you hear what I said?" She uncrossed her legs; her feet brushed the concrete floor. "We've just got to move. Mrs. Clark's is the only place right now. It won't be so bad."

Besides the no-smoking rule, Mrs. Clark had a midnight curfew. I remembered that she collected everything. Teacups, sea glass, dolls, wind chimes, and thimbles with tiny pictures on them. Grace said she was a pack rat. Everything we owned could fit into our two brown suitcases and the trunk of the Dodge. She made me comb my hair and wash my hands before dinner. The three of us sat around her paisley-print tablecloth lined with fringe while Mrs. Clark bowed her head in prayer. Some nights, Mrs. Clark might corner Grace into listening to her play the piano. Grace would find reasons to make ten trips to the bathroom. Once, I caught her blowing smoke out the bathroom window. She said she felt like a "goddamn teenager," stormed into her bedroom, and slammed the door. I had to take her place on Mrs. Clark's flowered love seat and listen to her play "My Hopes Have Departed Forever."

"This is the last time you'll change schools. We'll get our own place by spring."

I saw the other side of the billboard, an advertisement for Ojai's community hospital. Two cartoon doctors held babies in their arms, one white, the other black. I could dial D-E-L-I-V-E-R if I wanted to call them. I thought I might try it when we got to Mrs. Clark's.

"Are we going to Mrs. Clark's now?"

"No. To Al's."

"Why?"

"To get our things."

"Why?"

"I told him not to be there. He better not be."

She said it with an edge, one that told me she still had steam. Whatever they had fought about the night before wasn't finished. If Al was there, I wasn't sure if we'd make it to Mrs. Clark's. Grace liked to pack and argue at the same time. She'd slam drawers, fold her clothes better than usual, and sit on her stuffed brown suitcase, trying to zip it, yelling, "You don't care! All you think about is yourself!" until my father, or Steve, or John, or maybe even Al, grabbed her arm, pulled her off the suitcase, and begged her to stay.

Grace switched lanes to pass a blue Volvo on the highway. I knew she hoped Al would be at the apartment. She blew smoke from her cigarette out her nose.

We passed the fruit stand at the corner and drove down the long street to Al's apartment. Grace pulled the Dodge up to the curb, the front tire rubbing against it. She threw the car into park and glanced at Al's parking space next to the building. It was empty.

"Come on, J.D.," she said, yanking the door handle. "Let's go pack our things."

I put my book on the dash and followed Grace up the tall, dark steps that led to the front door of the apartment. I knew a dragon who drank from the swimming pool of the building when the superintendent was away on an errand. I'd put my toe into the hot jets of water pulsing through the pool when the dragon dropped his nose in for a drink. He needed plenty of water from breathing all that fire.

Before we reached the top of the steps, Grace stopped in her tracks. "That sonofabitch," she said. I peeked under her left arm to see what she was looking at. Sitting in front of the closed door were our two brown suitcases, the exercise bike Al had bought her for Christmas, and the stuffed dinosaur I had gotten from the museum in San Diego. One of the dinosaur's eyes was missing. It was loose, and I had meant to glue it. It must have fallen off when Al put it outside.

Grace walked up the rest of the stairs faster. She moved the exercise bike aside and wrenched the doorknob. Locked. We always locked the door. I didn't know why Grace thought it would be open. She gave the door a shove with her shoulder, then hit her fist against it.

"Why don't you use the key?" I asked.

Grace turned around and kicked the exercise bike on its side. It crashed loudly, and the timer bell rang like a damaged horn. Mr. Potts downstairs probably heard it.

"I can't use the key because I threw it at Al last night." Grace sat down on one of the suitcases and put her face in her hands. "God," she said through her fingers, "everything's screwed up."

It was quiet for a moment. I heard someone dive into the pool. I heard the fat kid riding his Big Wheel through the cars in the parking lot.

Then I heard Grace laughing. At first I thought she was crying, and she might have been, but when she pulled her face from her hands, she was laughing.

"I was just thinking," she said between laughs. "Remember that shirt Mrs. Clark made me? I gave it to Al to tie around his head during his bowling tournament. What if she wants to make me another one?"

I laughed too. "Ask her to play the piano."

Grace giggled until her eyes watered. I stopped and grew watchful, her laugh confusing me with its lack of shape and ending. Her thin shoulders stuck out of her tank top and jumped up and down with her laughter. Her curly blond hair fell across her face like a curtain. She grabbed the bottom of her loose skirt, wiped the tears from the corners of her eyes. She looked at me.

"J.D.," she said, "do you think I'm a weird mom?"

Her question surprised me. I looked at her bony knees peeking out from under her hiked-up skirt. I noticed the little scab on her knee, tough and hard and ready to peel off.

"Oh, never mind," Grace said, getting up from the brown suitcase and lifting it by the handle. "Don't answer that. I don't want to know."

I was going to tell her she wasn't a weird mom, but I was glad she told me not to answer. I wasn't sure if I'd be telling the truth.

I grabbed the smaller suitcase, put the stuffed dinosaur under my arm. We walked down the steps, our suitcases banging against the walls, and passed the mailbox with our names posted under Al's: Grace Caple/J.D. Mulroy. I lost my grip on the suitcase. It hit the floor. I picked it up and switched the dinosaur to the other arm.

Grace was already at the Dodge. She opened the trunk.

"Grace!" I shouted. "Aren't we going to put the exercise bike in there?"

"No," she said. "I'm leaving that here. I never used it anyway."

She threw the large brown suitcase on top of the spare tire. She got into the Dodge, started it, and raised the volume of the radio. I swung my small suitcase into the trunk next to the big one. The dinosaur fell to the ground beneath the chrome bumper. It looked up at me with one black, oval eye. I decided I was through with dinosaurs and didn't pick it up. I shut the trunk as hard as I could.

I got into the Dodge. It screeched and left the curb. I whipped around in my seat, stared out the back window at the stuffed animal on the pavement, bouncing in the smoke and dust.

⚸ ⚸ ⚸

"I have just one thing to say." Mrs. Clark greeted us at the front door. Her hands were on her hips. She wore a white silk robe printed with two large red flowers spreading from her waist to her underarms, up around the collar. She looked like a red crab standing on her spindly old legs. "The man never deserved both of you, not even one of you. I won't say any more," she said, twisting around, one hand waving in the air.

Grace and I stood in the doorway, gripping our suitcases. We watched Mrs. Clark amble through the side door to the garage, where she kept a second refrigerator, stocked with sodas. The door swung closed behind her.

She once told me that her secret dream was to be a clothes designer. The last time we'd lived with her, she had made Grace a long shirt with a cat embroidered on it. She took one of Grace's silver cat earrings to use as a pattern. Grace walked around for two weeks with one earring hanging from her ear so she wouldn't forget Mrs. Clark had the other half of her favorite pair. When the shirt was finished, Grace wore it over a black leather miniskirt to make Mrs. Clark feel good. Mrs. Clark wouldn't let her out the door that night until she'd fixed Grace's hair and put makeup on her. Grace came out of the bathroom with a face I hardly recognized. "Now, you go out there and get a man," Mrs. Clark had said to her, smiling with approval.

I followed Grace down the hallway. Her shoulders were slumped. She carried her suitcase as if it were growing heavier. It hit the wall and bounced against her knee. "Shit," she said under her breath.

I glanced back at Mrs. Clark's living room. It hadn't changed. The china windmill still sat on the old Magnavox hi-fi. Her collection of cups and saucers from every town, city, country she visited was arranged in alphabetical order on small shelves along the walls. Dark, thick paintings of foreign streets hung imperially in bulky gold frames. And the oriental rug she had brought back from China spread across the center of the room as her prized spoil. "J.D.," she had whispered one night after several glasses of sherry, "you've never seen so many bicycles."

We passed Mrs. Clark's room, where a lace sachet filled with crushed rose petals hung from her door. She kept her door closed, and I had to knock if I needed to tell her something. She'd always ask who was there, even though she knew I was the only one in the house with her.

The two bedrooms at the end of the hall were ours, directly across from each other. Grace took the one on the right. It had belonged to Bill, Mrs. Clark's deceased husband. She'd left it the way it had been the day he died: a bed, a dresser, a dark wood desk, and a plaid bedspread; it was as spare as Mrs. Clark's room was fussy. The phone was gone from the desk, but the desk blotter was still there, with Bill's faded blue ink doodles swirling across paper that had yellowed and puckered.

Bill died at his desk the year he retired. Mrs. Clark said he'd died from something akin to crib death: "He just stopped breathing air, like an infant in its first month." She hadn't said any more than that, as if it were a satisfactory explanation for a man's sudden passing.

Grace heaved her suitcase onto the bed. The old mattress creaked. She looked around the room once, went to the window, and threw the curtain back, desperate for air. Outside the window stood a wall.

"The room's the same," I said.

"The phone's gone." She turned toward me and rubbed her brow impatiently. "Why don't you unpack your things," she said, in a way that told me she wanted to be alone.

"Are you unpacking yours?" I wanted to make sure she wasn't going anywhere, slipping out when I wasn't looking.

"In a few minutes," she said testily.

I walked across the hall slowly, looking back once. The pink quilt and white bedpost peeked through the doorway. Nothing had changed. I felt angry again that I had to take this room. Grace had said it made her feel dizzy and she couldn't last a day in it. The ballerina posters still hung on the wall, and *Little Women* stood between two bookends, along with a Nancy Drew story, on the white bookshelf.

The room had belonged to Becky, the girl Mrs. Clark and Bill had adopted years earlier. The story went that when Becky was old enough, she decided to look for her real parents, found her dad in a trailer park near the ocean with seven adopted Vietnamese children, and decided to stay with him to help out. It was another strange story Mrs. Clark told to explain the gaping loss of people in her life. I understood there were some things you just had to have enough sense not to question.

I set my suitcase on the floor. The bed was too high; there were two tiny steps to reach the top. I looked around the room, sat on the step stool, and kicked my suitcase so it fell over flat.

The sound of Mrs. Clark's sandals *thump-thumped* down the hall.

"J.D.," she said, gripping the doorframe as if it held her up, "want a cream soda? I brought one in from the garage. Now, you know they're special, so don't say no."

"Sure."

She looked around the room for a minute, then at the bedroom with me in it. I suddenly felt like a part of Mrs. Clark's design. "Back in your old room again," she said. "We'll have fun, you and me. I've still got the games in the garage. The Parcheesi, and what's that other one?"

"Monopoly."

"That's it. The one with the fake bills."

I looked down at my feet and wondered how I'd stand this when Grace went out.

"Tillie missed you. She's waiting for you out back. Why don't you take your soda outside?"

I slid off the stool, stretched my arms above my head. Mrs. Clark went into Grace's room. I heard her whisper, "What'd he do to you? He didn't strike you, did he?"

"No, he'd never hit me, " Grace said loudly, exasperated.

I went out to the kitchen and found my cream soda in a plastic cup. I slid open the screen door to the back porch. Tillie squiggled her long body around, her tail wagging in the direction opposite her head. Her little body was a wavering line. Her two front paws jumped an inch off the ground. I reached down, stroked her on the head; her eyelids pulled back from her bulging eyes.

"Catch any birds?"

She whimpered after me as I cut across the lawn. I sat down on a large gray boulder Mrs. Clark had set in the middle of her garden. Tillie was smashing the pansies.

I lifted her onto my lap, and she licked my face until I couldn't stand it anymore. A bird flew over us. Tillie soared off my lap after it. I watched her stubby legs swim across the grass.

The sun was setting behind the shingled roofs of houses. I took a long drink of my soda, the bubbles sweet and good. I heard some scratching on the other side of the wall. I thought it was the Beckers' dog, but then the scratching climbed the wall and the sandy-colored bangs of the Beckers' granddaughter reached the top. Her whole face appeared—the turned-down nose and round cheeks. Her hair was longer than before; her legs were longer too.

"Oh, you're here," she said. "I was going to steal some strawberries."

"Go ahead."

"You won't tell?"

"No."

She climbed over the wall, making sure to pull the bottom of her purple shorts down so nothing showed. She had a new pair of sneakers with neon orange trim.

"Been to Flagstaff?" she asked. Her sneakers hit the ground. She smacked her hands together to clean off the dirt.

"No."

"I have. Grandma and Grandpa took me over spring break. I saw this place where a meteor hit the earth. A big, giant crater about the size of Mrs. Clark's house."

"So?"

"You wouldn't say that if you saw it."

Something about Debbie had me poised for competition. The last time I saw her, she'd been getting off the school bus, pretending to be a horse, galloping to her grandparents' home, jumping hedges and whinnying. She had a backyard filled with imaginary horses, names for all of them, a feeding schedule written down in a notebook. I told her it was stupid, but secretly I wanted a backyard for my own imaginary world, one I could count on when I got back from school.

Debbie crouched over the strawberry plants. Her fingers searched through the little green leaves for ripe strawberries, sweet and red. She chose them carefully, putting them into a plastic baggie. She would take them home, sprinkle them with sugar, and eat them whole.

"When did you get here?"

"Today," I said.

"Your mom break up with another boyfriend?"

"Something like that."

Debbie held her baggie up to the pink light of the sunset, examining her strawberries.

"Did you like him?"

"He was all right."

I walked to the edge of the lawn, away from Debbie. I thought about the time Al took me to bowl. It was an early Saturday morning, the lanes were empty, and we sat in the alley coffee shop before we got started. I sat across the table from Al but never looked at his face. He drank cup after cup of black coffee; I played with the soggy Froot Loops in my bowl. It was the end of our first week living with Al, and although everything had gone well, I still didn't want to know him, fought hard to forget his name.

When Al finished his last cup of coffee, we walked down the steps to the front counter, where Al asked the man for a small pair of bowling shoes. They were red, white, and blue, with Velcro straps. Al and I sat down on a bench. He removed his own pair of bowling shoes from the black sport sack he always carried.

I couldn't remember much more of that morning: if we had a good time, if I learned to bowl, or if Al and I even played. What I did remember were his hands. Al had large hands, and when they reached down to help me with my shoes, I looked over his back at his bowling ball to see how big the holes were. His fingers worked my shoe straps—strong, sure fingers so different from the thin, shy ones of my mother, the ones that taught me double knots and buckles.

Tillie lay in the shade of a small lime tree, chewing hard on the end of a stick. I tried to take it from her, but she ran with it clenched in her teeth, her ears bouncing.

I noticed Mrs. Clark had not trimmed the ivy growing on the far cinder-block wall; the spade-shaped leaves and curly-haired vines clung to cracks and pulled them wider apart. I set my glass on the ground, stuck my toe in a crack, and lifted myself up onto the wall. From that spot, I could see the stitched-together backyards of many houses. Pools and barbecues. A swing set. Fences cutting them up into neat squares. Mrs. Fuesuelo's zucchini garden. The Starks' new satellite dish.

"When did the Starks get the dish?" I asked Debbie.

"A few months ago. They get a station from Russia. Alaska too."

I swung around, faced Debbie, my feet dangling below me. She was bending over, picking strawberries again, her loose top hanging down so that I could see her nipples, two shiny copper pennies.

It felt strange to look. She could have been my little sister. I always thought of her as the Beckers' grandchild. Yet I kept looking. Her long hair swung with the movement of her arms, brushing her collarbone. I could see the outline of her breasts beginning to fill her shirt, growing, eventually filling a bra like Grace's with a bow at its center. I stared and imagined until she lifted her head, swung the baggie up, twisted the top into a tight knot.

"You're still so skinny," she said, glancing at me sitting on top of the wall, then back at her baggie, as if I didn't warrant more attention. "Your knees look like chicken bones."

I stared down at my knees sticking out from my khaki shorts, lifted my eyes quickly, mad that she had gotten me to look. I was skinny, I knew that. Many things didn't agree with me. I was allergic to milk, juniper bushes, feather pillows, and cats. I avoided these things after learning they made me wheeze and tripled the size of my eyelids. I jumped down from the wall, swiped up my glass. "Your grandma's calling you," I said.

"No, she's not."

"Mrs. Clark's coming."

Debbie quickly looked over her shoulder and clenched her baggie. She dashed over the wall, the black treads of her sneakers flashing past my eyes. She hopped down to the other side, the red baggie following her, held high by her lifted arm. "Got 'em," she called from the other side, "and I guess you don't want any."

"That's right," I called back, though the thought of the sweet sugar on the fresh berries made my mouth water.

I walked back to the screen door and stopped to look at the concrete wall between us. How long would I be here this time? I wondered, though I knew I couldn't ask. Would I see Debbie again? Did I want to?

Tillie dropped her stick and followed me to the screen door. I slid it open and stared into Mrs. Clark's kitchen, which looked dark and gloomy after the bright sun outside. I felt Tillie brush my leg as she waited for me to be the first to go in.

"Tillie," I said to her pleading eyes, "did you miss me?"

The Dragon

———————

It is a very large dragon, he decides, who can breathe water and fire. He lies on his back in bed, the pale yellow sheet just under his nose so he can breathe through his nostrils and make it flutter, or through his mouth so it billows.

He stares at the stucco ceiling above him. If he does this long and hard enough, the pits and dots, shades and shadows of white, turn into a kingdom, creatures, mountains, streams, and a dragon, a very large one who can breathe water and fire.

His body is weightless in the cool bed. The outlines of his arms, his legs, his kneecaps, and his feet beneath the folds of yellow are the clouds, suns, discs, and planets of his imaginary sky. His raised knee shifts below the sheet, and the sun is setting over the kingdom. The dragon stirs in his cave. His left arm slices across the mattress, and an evening breeze enchants the land.

The dragon's eyes are open. He turns in his cave, the long, serpentine tail uncoiling behind him in a movement of dots. Stretching his neck past the opening to the cave, he blinks his large eyes in the nighttime darkness and he sees. He sees the stream of light cast from the moon, a perfectly round moon. He jiggles his knee, the sheet rustles, and the thin yellow tent cascades from the top of his kneecap into a pool of shimmering light at the base of the dragon's two front feet.

The dragon lifts one clawed foot, checks its bottom. Is the light from the feet or the moon? He looks at the moon, back at his foot, the graceful arc of his neck a thin line of stucco.

His large tail rises and hits the floor of his cave with a frustrated, thunderous punch. The cave rocks; shadows play with the crisscross of light hitting the wall: first a man with horns, then a mammoth with shoes, then a spear without a point. An owl looks down from where he sits on a shaking branch. Shaking pine cones. It is a tall sequoia; its needles glisten.

He laughs and jiggles the moon to taunt the dragon. The world above his bed sways, floats, moves closer. The sheet around his mouth puffs with the dragon's breath.

A door closes outside, footsteps approach the house, but he does not remove his eyes from the ceiling, the dragon, the owl, the moon. He hears the front door open, the sound of flat and beaten soles dragging farther away, across the carpet to the kitchen, the click-open of the cupboard for a glass. His moon no longer beams, and the dragon leaves his cave, his tail sliding on the ground in crescent waves behind him. The refrigerator opens—the pop of an aluminum lid.

The sheet rises and falls slowly. Everything is still; he hears only the sound of the dragon's breath. The dragon looks both ways and crosses. He leaves tracks in the soft earth beneath him, pointed and round, four claw marks each imprinted on stucco.

He bends his elbows, pulling his arms up, and his palms face forward beneath the sheet. He can feel the light fabric held up by his fingertips, resting on them smoothly, as if touching glass, clear and beautiful glass. He pushes one finger forward, then another, shooting stars breaking through. They unfurl themselves across the sky, draping the dragon in tiny sparkles. And the dragon stops in his tracks, stares at the moon, the full moon, playing another trick on him with not a beam, but a shower, of light.

The dragon pulls his tail straight, lifts it from the ground, and in one giant motion swats at the moon with a force so strong, it raises his hind legs an inch off the soft earth.

His knee glides to the right beneath the yellow sheet, the moon escaping the slap. He laughs at the dragon, sends another star from the tip of his index finger through the vast evening sky. The rain of brilliant dots falls slowly, gently, down the dragon's raised face. Softly. Footsteps grope down the hall, grow louder; he can hear them sniffing, like tracking dogs, past the space beneath the door and then grow softer. Thistle closes behind them.

He lowers his fingertips from the sheet. The owl adjusts his footing on the branch. The dragon stares with wonder at the quiet sky, anticipating the next shot of light from the moon. And across the hall, a window winces shut. The sound drifts through the air, under his door, beneath the needles of his tree, the underside of his owl, who flutters his wings, blinks his eyes. His lids dip; the owl blurs. On his bed he falls asleep. His knees float beneath the sheet, through the calendar days of his world, his moon from full to half, then to crescent.

Robbie Released

When Robbie E. Mullen came to the door, Isabel was watching a talk show featuring twin sisters who had swapped their husbands without their knowing. Now the couples were living in neighboring towns. One sister liked her new spouse; the other didn't. The one who didn't said she missed little things, like her husband's remembering the day of their anniversary. On the show the day before was a man who had eaten an automobile. "Truth," the host liked to remind his viewers, "is stranger than fiction." Isabel always nodded her head in agreement.

She began watching these shows—there were two in a row—after her neighbor Lillian Venesi had answered *The Maury Povich Show*'s request for women whose best friends were taking away their husbands. The whole town watched. Lillian appeared on the show via satellite, and while she talked, a caption appeared at the bottom of the screen, reading, "Lillian Venesi: Believes Best Friend Is Stealing Her Husband."

This was the closest anyone from Buckeye, California, had ever come to celebrity. At first, Isabel had watched Lillian tell her story with curious disgust, but by the end of the episode she'd become envious of her neighbor and wished that *she* had been Lillian Venesi, beamed across the empty desert to the entire country.

Isabel turned the TV off reluctantly. She thought the knock on the door was the repairman from Whirlpool. Her refrigerator was broken, and splayed across the kitchen counter was the spoiled food she meant to throw away as soon as the show was over.

She opened the door, and her hands, puffy from summer heat, flew above her raspberry-hued hair. "Robbie," she gasped, nearly choking on his name.

Her brother had been in prison for armed robbery of a convenience store in Nevada. He had pointed a Smith & Wesson at a trembling salesclerk and taken $200 in cash and a box of baseball cards with bubble gum. Isabel had thought he had seven more months to serve. She'd been keeping track by the "America the Beautiful" calendar she'd tacked to the wall of her pantry closet. On February 23, below the picture of the Grand Canyon, she'd written in her small handwriting, "Robbie released."

"Surprised?" he said in a flat tone. The new feature on his thin face was an unkempt, goldish beard that reminded her of a horn instrument. He wore the same black-rimmed glasses, a duffel bag slung over one shoulder, blue jeans torn at the knees. He had the mannerisms of a lizard perched on a hot rock, not bothered by the heat, surveying his environment slowly.

At Robbie's side, a giant, hairy white dog panted and drooled over his sandals. Isabel flattened against the wall as Robbie strode past. She felt panic run through her; she'd often wondered if her brother knew who'd turned him in.

His eyes scanned the table of refrigerator wreckage—the spoiled milk and ground beef, an old box of melted Fudgsicles.

"What's all this?"

"The refrigerator's not working," she said.

"*Nothing* works in this town," he said flatly.

A person could do a lot worse than Buckeye, Isabel thought, and for that brief moment she tried fervently to believe it.

"You got my package, Robbie?" she asked, with more anxiety in her voice than she'd wished to give away. She had sent two dozen oatmeal cookies to the Lovelock Correctional Center, wrapped carefully in sets of six, the box padded with plenty of paper.

He went to the kitchen sink and filled a bowl of water for the dog. Then he took a can of soup from the pantry, opened it, and spooned it into his mouth, cold.

"I got it," he said, "after the COs searched it and ate the cookies."

"Oh," Isabel said, shaking her head, "that's terrible. How'd you get out so soon?"

He racked the spoon against the can's ridges. The noise reminded her of a tin cup rattling across bars. She wondered how Robbie had outwitted his keepers. Had he played the wrongly accused? Or the remorseful convict?

On Robbie's face was that familiar, crooked grin. "Good behavior," he drawled, confirming her worst suspicion.

⌘ ⌘ ⌘

Before Isabel saw Lillian Venesi on TV, she had seen Lillian most often from down the block, saying goodbye to relatives on holidays, in the seat of her departing or arriving car, or picking weeds around her mailbox in fuzzy red slippers.

She hadn't known Lillian Venesi very well, though they had lived near each other for close to five years. It was a small town, and old alliances hung thick. The Venesis were newcomers. No one moved to Buckeye anymore, the townspeople decided, without a sinister motive.

No one believed, for instance, that the Venesis had inherited their old, vacant brick house from an aunt. One person said they were drug runners. Another said they were tax evaders. Still another thought they were in the witness protection program, their true identities wiped clean.

The last was the story that captured Isabel's imagination most. In her daydreams she was in the program herself, secretly shuttled away from her husband and friends, a new haircut, a new wardrobe, a new life in a city with buses and taxicabs, people coming and going. Then, after a year or so, her husband would arrive to search for her. She'd have a chance encounter with him on a train or a congested street. It would be rushed and sweetened by danger. He would beg for answers she couldn't give him. She would meet him in restaurants with foreign names.

Isabel tried hard to convince herself that her life was no less interesting than her neighbor's. She had a job as a manicurist at the Nail Hut. She had no formal training, but she knew how to deal with unruly cuticles and had learned to French-tip fingernails from a *Redbook* magazine article.

She was grateful for her job. The majority of business at the Nail Hut came from retired mothers in search of social outlets. Isabel filed their chipped, damaged nails into smooth ovals. She buffed away the old layers turned yellow from fatigue and housework. Then she painted their nails in shades called Luminous Plum and Dinner Party Red.

Sometimes Isabel's customers would bring in home-baked cookies—buttery shortcake or chocolate fudge—which they would eat with decadent care, their fingers extended so the polish wouldn't smudge. At lunchtime she might gather with a group around the TV to watch Maury Povich strut in front of a live audience.

"Haven't you ever wondered," Isabel once asked a friend, "what it's like to be on one of those shows?"

The buoyant hosts began circling in her dreams at night. One, a glossy Oprah look-alike, peered into her living room and whispered family secrets into the microphone.

The Nail Hut was in a neatly painted pink shack that stood next to a drive-through liquor store. During the day, the liquor store looked like a boarded-up outhouse, but by four o'clock the window opened and Sal, a salt-and-pepper-haired man who sometimes wore a blue cap, set his elbows on the window ledge. By 4:15, there were at least three cars in line.

One of the cars was always Isabel's husband, Martin. He bought his fifth of whiskey and took it to share with his buddies around a forest-green pool table or in front of a wide-screen TV after work. He had to unwind, he told Isabel, after a day of peddling fertilizer to irritable farmers in distant counties.

Isabel was sure they sat around, a group of post-middle-aged men, grunting and huffing about their politics and sports. The young men had begun to leave Buckeye when they graduated from high school. They moved to glittering cities whose names roared in Isabel's ears like the passing 18-wheelers on the interstate: Los Angeles, Phoenix, Seattle. Her own two sons had left town as soon as they could. One worked in construction in Phoenix; the younger one was something called a gaffer in Hollywood.

She was reluctant to admit that Buckeye had become what her sons called a "hick town." The Sears Roebuck no longer delivered; there were no new, shiny neon shopping malls; and the peach farmers, whose abounding yields had once been the town's glory, either had moved or were slowly dying off. The few shopkeepers who eked out a living now catered to tourists who came in late Friday afternoons on their way to the emerging gambling oasis in Laughlin, Nevada. They loaded Indian moccasins and peach jam in jars with fake old-fashioned labels into their foreign cars before they sped through the invisible town to the highway lined with crooked Joshua trees.

The empty house. The *tick-tock*ing of the clock. Isabel knew women could do strange things when their children left home.

The Farnsworth woman, for instance, had lived on the edge of town in a shingle-roofed house with an orderly yard. No broken-down tractors there, or discarded TV sets. Her three children had gone on to respectable lives. But one year, after the youngest son left, she drove her car right through the house as if it were the on-ramp to the interstate and never returned.

Isabel went to see the Farnsworth home after the accident. A gaping hole exposed it like the inside of a dollhouse. Part of the roof had collapsed onto the kitchen sink. Isabel had turned from the house quickly, feeling shame rise across her cheeks, and thinking then that no one needed to come so close to the source of another's desperation.

⌘ ⌘ ⌘

Robbie finished the soup and tossed the empty can onto the counter. Isabel eyed the enormous dog, which flattened onto the cool linoleum floor, panting heavily. She felt its black-eyed stare. "Where'd you get the dog?" she asked, searching for harmless conversation.

"Roxy. She was next to a Winnebago in New Mexico," Robbie said. "I took her as a good omen."

Leave it to Robbie, she thought, to steal a huge white dog his first days out of prison. Her brother had never been particularly smart. She could always tell when he lied to their father. Once, he had stolen one of Daddy's checks, thinking that if he took one with a high number from the bottom of the stack, it would be a long time before Daddy discovered it.

Robbie could always convince Daddy that a little more attention was all he needed. Their mother died when they were young. Their father, who was a truck driver, spent what little free time he had trying to "straighten out" Robbie.

When Robbie finally got expelled from school, Daddy took him along on truck trips while Isabel remained at home with holy

Aunt Helen, who scribbled Christian proverbs on scraps of paper she slipped into Isabel's knapsack.

Robbie wore the same smirk on his face whenever he returned from a long trip with glass jars that he lined his windowsills with, like colorful postcards. Gray-green pollywogs in murky water, Oregon frogs whose breath steamed the glass, wilted lilacs from the Midwest, and, once, a tiny turtle from Washington that had fascinated Isabel the most. She had peered into the jars as if they were small windows to the outside world. Green, lush, and alive.

On the morning of her tenth birthday, Robbie gave her one of the magical jars, and Isabel looked in with delight to find a little speckled turtle.

"You can have it," Robbie said, brushing past her. "It was already dead when I found it."

Now, here was Robbie in her kitchen, still going about his business as if she weren't there. He slid the duffel bag off his shoulder so he could fill it with soup cans, her diet sodas, and a box of gingersnaps. When he had finished, his fixed gaze gave her a start.

"Give me the brooch," he said. He stretched his palm out toward her.

"The brooch?" she repeated, stalling for time. It was a bar of pure gold with a large diamond and two pearls that had once been their mother's. Daddy had given it to Isabel in a worn blue velvet box. It was the sole memento Isabel had from her mother. The one thing she'd been given that Robbie had not.

"Don't take me for a jackass," Robbie hissed. "I think we both know why you owe me that pin."

Isabel blinked hard, as if she were seeing the two-headed chicken at the county fair. She knew he would pawn the brooch for cash. She'd never had her mother's brooch appraised, but she was sure Robbie had done his calculations. She'd never even thought to wear it, sitting in its plush box like a totem in her bedroom. It had never occurred to her that a monetary value could be placed on the pin, and this astonished her more than the news that he knew she had turned him in.

"Robbie Mullen," she said, her voice a sanctimonious accusation, "what would Father say?"

"Father," he said, his voice dry as the wind, "is dead."

✖ ✖ ✖

In the days following Lillian Venesi's appearance on TV, Isabel had watched her use her fame like blue-chip stamps. She traded it in for free meals at the Cactus Café, and the owner of the Nail Hut invited her in for a free manicure. She became an instant celebrity overnight. People in town began to remember Lillian's dear old aunt. Her adulterous husband had not shown his face around town. Someone heard he was cooking dinner for Lillian every night.

When outsiders came through town, they were invariably asked if they had seen the show. If they hadn't, the story would be repeated to them in a cautionary tone suggesting the townspeople had inside knowledge that scandal often lurked closer than they knew.

But what had struck Isabel the most was the sound of applause. She heard it every time she walked into Ned's Grocery, where a small crowd of people huddled around the TV hooked up to the counter so those who missed Lillian Venesi could see the taped show again and again. Lillian's inflamed face filled the screen. It wasn't her story so much as the fact that she was on TV and came from the very same town that got everyone so excited. When the host of the show mentioned Buckeye by name, the crowd whooped and hollered and Ned, who held the remote control, rewound to hear it one more time.

Isabel was the one who had given Lillian Venesi her complimentary manicure. She painted Lillian's fingernails a sleek shade of red, feeling like the dutiful subject before the queen.

Lillian set her pear-shaped rear back in the chair. Her broad chest rose and fell with each breath. She'd begun dressing more elegantly since the show, as if she had an image to uphold, royal and vindicated. Isabel felt strangely diminished by her, though she reminded herself that this was the same woman she'd seen pick weeds in fuzzy slippers.

"He's been sleeping on the couch," Lillian said loudly, so the whole shop could hear. She perched one hand over Isabel's and rested the other on her hip. "By all I can tell, my devil friend Julie's pregnant and she's left town."

Isabel had watched the women in the shop straining to hear more on that detail. Julie Rayburn, after all, had been one of their own. Her family had run the town gas station for three generations. Julie had been the first to invite Lillian to a Nail Hut luncheon, quietly befriending her and easing her into the female fold gathered around the TV with aluminum foil and cotton on their fingertips. Julie and Lillian became good friends. The friendship gave Julie a boost of confidence—poor, gun-shy soul—to start dating after her fiancé had left her at the altar many years earlier. But she went too far, according to the Nail Hut women, when she hung streamers for the peach fair in a red stretch miniskirt in full view of the townsmen, who gaped like hungry birds. If only Julie hadn't done that, Isabel thought, while buffing Lillian's nails, she would have remained in their protective fold. Then she might never have gotten involved with Lillian Venesi's husband.

Thinking about that now, Isabel felt a pang of regret for Julie. But she kept those feelings to herself. She even caught herself wondering what Julie would do now.

Where had she gone, pregnant and alone? Had Lillian's husband even given her a dime?

✕ ✕ ✕

Isabel had made the phone call.

She had watched the police artist's sketch of her brother's face change with the aid of computer graphics. First a mustache, then none. Then heavy features and long hair and no glasses. His changing appearance seemed to fill all the chance years she'd seen him, as if she were looking through a dusty, forgotten photo album.

Crime Stoppers' 800 number trailed beneath Robbie's chin like skywriting: "If you or anyone you know," the narrator's voice boomed, "have information leading to the arrest and conviction . . ."

She had called to Martin, while poking a finger at the screen, "It's him, Marty! It's him!"

"That's not Robbie," Martin said, rattling the newspaper from his reclining chair. He had arrived at such a state of blissful indifference that he no longer even rolled his eyes. But Isabel knew it was Robbie, and when she lifted the receiver, she had already talked herself into believing she was doing what was best for her wayward brother.

Events work in mysteriously linked ways, Isabel thought now, as she sat down on a chair before her brother as calmly as she could. She might not have seen the show if she hadn't come home early. But there she had been, fixing two plates of fried chicken and mashed potatoes, when Robbie's face had flashed on the screen.

"Do you remember," she said, as slowly as she could, "the story behind Mother's brooch?" She knew she'd get nowhere if Robbie figured out how desperate she was to hold on to it. Her childhood instincts reminded her that he had always responded to panic in others with a peculiar zeal.

The story had been told to Isabel many times. When money

76

was tight, their father had taken the brooch to a pawn shop. Their mother had cried and cried. When money was still scarce, the brooch had been sold, leaving an empty spot in the display case. Then their mother developed a limp, dragging her lame leg across the carpet like a ball and chain. One day, their father came home with the brooch. He never told anyone how he'd recovered it. The missing part of the story remained, for Isabel, an enchanting mystery.

When she finished retelling the tale, Robbie's face became grim. She tried to read his expression. Had her account touched him or only triggered his disgust?

"You still believe that bullshit story?" he asked.

"That brooch was special to Mother, Robbie. Daddy told me that many times."

Robbie snickered. "Daddy gambled that brooch away. Just like he gambled almost everything he ever earned."

Isabel felt anger rising inside her. "Take that back, Robbie!" she snapped. She wanted to call him a no-good thief. She wanted to blurt out that when she had dialed, she had wondered what she would wear on TV. The royal-blue blouse—she looked good in blue—or the polka-dot dress she had worn to her sister-in-law's wedding. She had even practiced a few shocked facial expressions. Prison! Her own brother! "My own brother!" she mouthed, hand to chest, to the imaginary camera.

"*Crime Stoppers.* Please hold."

"I know who that man is," she had blurted into the phone.

The operator sighed, his voice dropping to the bottom of a well. "Which one?"

"The robber."

"The computer thief or the convenience-store thief?"

"The convenience-store thief," Isabel said. Then she whispered into the phone, "He's my brother, from Buckeye, California."

For two months after Robbie was arrested, Isabel had waited for something to happen. She had looked outside the window of her stucco home whenever a truck or car passed, her hopes crushed with each pair of retreating taillights. The empty gravel road. Wind kicking up dust. There was no truck with a satellite dish on its roof. No van with a camera. Not even a phone call.

But at the end of the eleventh week, she had ripped open an envelope addressed to her. A red button fell out. "CRIME BUSTER!" it read in bold letters. The note with it said:

Dear Informant,
You have made a significant contribution to our society. The citizens of your country, along with the producers of *Crime Stoppers*, sincerely appreciate your efforts. Your vigilance helped us remove another criminal from the streets of our nation. Though we would like to have each and every one of our informants appear as a guest on an episode of *Crime Stoppers*, we regret that we do not have sufficient programming time. Please accept our CRIME BUSTER button as a token of our appreciation.

Isabel threw the button out her window and never told her husband or friends a thing about it. She had watched Lillian Venesi stick a FOR SALE sign in front of her house—she and her husband were moving to a townhouse in Las Vegas—after she got a book deal to write her story. Her husband had atoned for his wrongs and now gazed at his wife with adoring eyes.

"We'll never know," Isabel said to the women at the Nail Hut, as she looked over the rims of distressed cuticles, the outrage spread across her face as thick as liverwurst, "why some people's stories get picked for TV and others don't."

✳ ✳ ✳

Robbie strode to the bedroom as Isabel bolted after him. Conscience had never prevented him from getting what he wanted. What was she thinking? "You need money!" she yelled. "Don't take Mom's brooch. I'll give you money!"

But Robbie grabbed the velvet box resting on her dressing table and pulled the delicate brooch out of it. "How much do you think I can get for it?"

He stuffed it into his pocket and threw the box onto the floor. Isabel lunged for him, her ferocity primal and pure. She ripped and clawed at his jeans. They fell onto the giant white dog, who scrambled out from underneath them and lumbered down the hall. She hooked her fingers into his jeans pocket. He yelled at her to let go. But she was hanging on for the one thing she truly deserved.

Then, suddenly, Isabel reached back for Martin's bowling trophy that rested on the lower shelf. She raised her hand to strike him with it, and for a split second she had the feeling of being outside herself, as if she were watching this fight on TV. The canned sound of applause echoed in her head like chickens scrambling across the desert, leaving clouds of thick dust and feathers. *Isabel Dobson*, she heard the host announce, *murdered her own brother*. And then the TV screen went dark—a sudden, unmerciful black.

White Shoes

―――――

Gloria's mother stood before the mirror in the dimly lit foyer, adjusting the collar of her silk blouse. Gloria was twelve years old, a tomboy always in pants, her hair a sun-dried weed crawling down her back, yet she was interested in the precise way her mother fussed with herself. She laid the collar flat, stepped back from the mirror with her hand poised, cocked her head from side to side, appraised it, stepped forward to adjust it a different way. She repeated these steps until she got it right. Then she licked her index finger to smooth her black eyebrow into a careful arch.

It was the morning of Thanksgiving. Her mother fizzled like a steam iron preparing for social outings. Her anticipation impressed Gloria more than what she did to pretty herself before the mirror. Implied was the feeling that they were going to a big event, not just her ordinary uncle's house, but an event that would be remembered in family photographs for all time, and it filled her with a mixture of excitement and dread. At her uncle's would be the standard turkey and gravy, along with the Latino sides of mole and Spanish rice that he added to the traditional American feast. And there would be more, a kind of pageant, a display of their success and how they were thriving as first-generation immigrants with second-generation families.

The formality of her mother's preparation hung like a weighted backpack on her shoulders, aching to be cast off once they made their entrance at her uncle's house, took the photographs, and then, finally, relaxed. Gloria stood in the doorway, wearing her worn suede Wallabee shoes beneath a dress that scratched at the neck.

"Take them off, Gloria," her mother said over her shoulder.

She looked down at her comfortable choice. "Why?"

"You know why. You think I don't know? They're beneath the coffee table. You hid them there."

Gloria dropped onto the couch. Beneath the table, a pair of new shoes lay like discarded relics from an uncool era. She rolled one of them onto its side with the toe of her Wallabee: a low-heeled pump in white patent leather that her mother had bought her for the occasion.

"Put them on," she said.

How could a pair of shoes be this bad? Gloria thought. She doubted that her aunt or uncle would be impressed by them. They lived in Los Angeles and had far better footwear options. Besides, she wondered, why the need to impress?

"They don't fit," she said, curling her big toe into a ball too fat to slide into the toe of the shoe.

Her mother froze before the mirror as if she'd just received word of a death in the family.

"You're a size four, aren't you?" she said.

Before Gloria could answer, her father came into the room to announce they were leaving. His gray hair was smoothed back, and he wore a golf shirt that stretched over his round belly. He looked like Bing Crosby after a day on the links. His Midwestern calm and casual manner were a sharp contrast to her mother's.

"You're wearing *that* shirt?" she said, her eyes sweeping over his striped polo.

"Yes, I am," he said. "What difference does it make? I'll put my sport coat over it."

Gloria shot up from the couch with a Wallabee in one hand, the other still on her foot.

"Let me see how they fit," her mother said, sadly refocused, crouching down to feel where Gloria's toe rested in the pump.

Her mother glanced up at her with a knowing look.

She reluctantly untied the second Wallabee. "I don't know why I have to wear these shoes. They're ugly!"

"Oh, let her wear her own shoes, Dolores," her father said. "Who are we trying to impress?"

"No one," she shot back. "But it's Thanksgiving, and I want her to look her best. I bought them for this trip."

"What trip, Dolores? It's your brother's house," her father mumbled.

"Maybe to you, John, it's just his house," her mother countered, as they walked to the front door, engaged now in each other, forgetting Gloria standing there with two different shoes in her hand. She quickly threw the pumps under the table and slipped on her worn Wallabees. She flipped off the light switch, leaving the ugly shoes in the dark and closing the door firmly behind her.

✕ ✕ ✕

Outside, the wide suburban streets lay empty, the neighbors' cars tucked safely in their driveways. In front of each house stood a tree the same as the next, lending the community a uniform look. The pale sidewalks were a thread tying all the homes together. A dog barked behind a fence across the street. Jimmy's bike was lying on the grass.

Her parents had bought the house in 1962. It was sown into the fields of the Conejo Valley, a good distance north of Los Angeles. Thousand Oaks was just catching up to the wave of suburban tract development after World War II. They had picked model number three, same as the Caugheys' house around the corner and the Wongs' house three doors down.

"Jimmy!" her mother hollered. Her voice echoed above the shingled rooftops, and soon they heard his voice call back from the dry field where the neighborhood children liked to explore snake holes or wild cattails that grew wild along the marsh. His shiny patent leather shoes popped down the concrete sidewalk. Dolores straightened his hair with saliva on her fingers. Jimmy's white button-down shirt was untucked, but he had somehow managed to keep himself neat.

"Why do we have to go?" Jimmy whined, sliding into the car next to Gloria.

"It's Thanksgiving, stupid."

"But Mrs. Collins said the story of the pilgrims and Indians isn't true."

"Oh, here we go," John said.

"Jimmy, straighten your shirt. We don't need to hear what Mrs. Collins thinks right now," Dolores said.

"But she's my teacher." Jimmy pouted in the back seat, his arms folded across his chest.

Gloria saw her friend Susie Wong bicycling up the street, and the field stretched golden past her window. She envied her friend, whose Chinese family didn't recognize the holiday. A bird stretched its wings and glided freely over the marsh. She looked out across the field longingly, her friend's legs pumping hard up the hill toward the orange grove.

❈ ❈ ❈

Uncle Eduardo stood on the front steps of his bungalow-style home. In the heart of Studio City, it had the low-roofed Hollywood glamour of an earlier era. His beige slacks were crisply pressed, a striped ascot knotted evenly at his neck. He took the same care that her mother did getting ready for these events. Tall, dark, and good-looking, he made sure he was always dressed for the occasion. Normally he would greet them at the door, requiring a hug and salutation before they entered the home. Yet today he looked serious, Gloria thought, like he had when he'd read the eulogy at her grandfather's funeral. He stood outside alone.

"What's with him?" her father asked as he pulled into the drive.

He moved slowly toward their car, his eyes reflecting some seriousness. Her mother quickly unlocked her door, sensing something was wrong, and jumped out. "*¿Qué pasa, Eduardo?*" she said, in the language she reserved for cursing or being with her family.

"*Alguien está aqui, Gloria.*"

As they moved toward the house together, her mother shot a look over her shoulder at John. "Let's stay in the car for a minute," he said. Gloria watched her mother walk into the house and then disappear inside. They were quiet for a while, staring at the closed front door and the large living room window that faced the drive. The hum of the highway was audible in the silence. Jimmy grew restless and fidgeted in his seat.

"Why don't we go in? Why do we have to wait here?"

Behind the sheer white curtains, Gloria saw a man move past the front window.

"Who's that, Daddy?" she asked.

"Don't know."

They watched the window for a while. "He said someone's here."

"Who said that?" her father asked.

"Uncle Eduardo."

When nothing happened, her father finally said, "Okay, let's go in. Lock your doors."

In the living room sat a man Gloria had never seen before. He wore a gray tweed coat with a shirt casually opened at the collar and loose, unpressed trousers. On his feet were shoes made of brown, unpolished leather. He was tall and heavyset, with a thick crop of graying hair. His hands gripped a glass that did not move from the table next to him.

Her uncle and mother sat in chairs opposite him, as if they were propped on a stage. Her mother's face was turned toward the dark entrance of the kitchen, though nobody was there. No one spoke or looked at anyone else. It was tense and silent. Gloria sensed that strange bond that occurs between adults when they don't want their children to know what's going on.

Her father ushered them down the hall into their aunt and uncle's bedroom, where Gloria's cousin Silvia reclined on the queen-size bed, watching a movie on television. The room was dark and cool. On the walls hung old movie posters and several framed photographs of the family.

Silvia stretched one tanned leg over the edge of the bed and let her sandal slide from her foot onto the floor. She wore a blue jean miniskirt and gold earrings. Gloria bent forward a little, suddenly self-conscious, hoping the hem of her dress would camouflage the shoes.

"Hi, kids," Silvia said. She was three years younger than Gloria but somehow always seemed three years older.

"That's good," her father said. "Watch the movie. Hello, Silvia." He left the room before she could answer.

Jimmy jumped onto the bed, relieved to be excused from adult business. The movie was a repeat of one they had seen before. A girl survived a plane crash in the Amazon jungle on Thanksgiving Day and struggled to make her way out. The same mesmerizing tussle with leeches and dark muddy river water.

"Who is he?" Gloria asked.

"Their brother, I guess," Silvia said. "I've never seen him before. I'm stuck in the 'no clue' room with you two."

"Brother? They don't have a brother," Gloria said.

"They do now." Silvia flopped over on her stomach. "He disappeared a long time ago."

From the bedroom, Gloria could hear the murmur of voices emanating from the living room. Their words rose and fell like tumbling water, drawing her to the secretive tone. She stepped into the hall for a moment, listening hard, but she could not make out a complete sentence, only insensible fragments and words.

She gazed over at the family photographs hanging on the wall. In one sepia portrait, her mother stood next to Uncle Eduardo, their serious teenage faces and dark, well-groomed hair. Her grandfather sat in a large wicker armchair; her grandmother stood stiffly on his left side. They all looked self-conscious, too precisely turned out and overdressed. No smiles for the photographer in those days, the portrait composed like a family document.

Her mother's voice rose. It sounded strained and angry, not upset in the way it did when Gloria or her brother was in trouble, but like it had when she'd lost a cherished ring her mother had given her.

Gloria moved closer. "What do you do up there in Seattle?" she heard her mother say.

The man's voice rang like the first speaker in a crowded auditorium. "I build things," he said.

Gloria stretched forward to take a peek at him, but she saw only the edge of her father's sweater, so she slid back.

"You build things?" her mother asked. "*¿Qué tipo de cosas?*"

"Dolores," her uncle said, in an attempt to calm her down.

"What? Tunnels and bridges? What things?"

Her father cleared his throat in the following silence.

"Office buildings, mostly," the man said.

"Well, you want to know what you didn't build?" Her mother's voice cracked. "*Una relación con tu familia.* You broke Mama's heart."

Her mother swept past the couch and walked out the front door. *She left!* Gloria had never heard her mother cry before. She knew something was terribly wrong. Gloria wanted to chase after her but stopped herself when she saw her father and aunt race out the door. She heard her father call, "Dolores!"

Now her uncle and the man were alone. Her mother had once told her that it was hard growing up in a home full of boys. She had said this as if she were talking about somebody else, a friend she had known. She said a girl would want to fit in with them, play the same games, but they would never let her.

"She's upset."

"She'll calm down," her uncle said, as he walked past the couch and out the front door to follow them. The man picked up his glass. The ice cubes clinked.

His eyes were blue. They were just like her grandmother's, more oval than almond shaped. He had her fair skin. The way he held his head and the shape of his cheekbones were familiar.

"What's your name?" the man said, spotting her in the hall. She stepped into the room.

"Gloria."

"You're Dolores's daughter?" He looked at her curiously.

She glanced down at her Wallabees. "Yes. Who are you?"

"I'm your mother's older brother. Steve."

Her uncle had changed his name from Eduardo to Edward so he could get work, he said, in a film industry that wanted to stereotype him as a Mexican gardener or street thug. She wondered what Steve's name had been. She gazed down at his dark, comfortably worn leather shoes. In the old photograph, her mother had worn ugly white patent leather shoes, the kind she had probably been forced to wear by her immigrant parents, who left Mexico in hopes that their children would grow up educated and affluent. Steve hadn't been in the photograph, but she was certain that if he had been, he'd have worn the same shiny black shoes Eduardo had on in the picture, unscuffed and polished. By the detached look in his eyes, she wondered if he would have wished to escape them too.

He glanced out the window. "Been to Disneyland?"

She kept gazing at his shoes. "Once."

"My kids are still dying to go."

He lifted his glass and took a drink. She wondered what it would be like to be his kids, to never see the family on holidays or go to funerals for dead relatives. She wondered if they knew about her and Jimmy and Silvia, young people just like them who were their cousins.

"How old are they?"

"Seventeen and nineteen."

"Do you have a different name?"

"I do. Esteban. I changed it after the war."

She said the name in her head twice. Difficult to pronounce. "Did you change it for work, like Uncle Eduardo did?" she asked.

"No, not initially. I just changed it to fit in better with my American wife, to be honest. But I guess you could say it helped with work too. Why not? Of course it did."

Gloria thought about his reason and tried to imagine his American wife. She envisioned a woman with blond hair pulled back from her face with a printed scarf. As soon as she did this, she realized it was silly. A movie-version picture. Her own father was American and looked nothing like a movie star. Her aunt was American too, slim like a dancer, but with raven hair.

"Are you here because it's Thanksgiving?" she asked.

"Sure. Smells good."

"Where are your kids?"

"Home with their mother."

"Where is your home?"

Before he could answer, her parents, aunt, and uncle came back through the door. Her mother was leading them as she walked briskly across the room to pick up her bag. She did not sit down or even talk to Steve. She caught Gloria standing in the hall, and her face softened for a moment. Gloria felt a wave of relief that she'd returned.

"Get your brother," she said. "We're leaving now."

"What?" my uncle exclaimed. "You're not staying for dinner? *¡Qué es esto!*" Gloria felt the same shock; they wouldn't eat Thanksgiving dinner? What was Steve thinking? Gloria wondered. Would she ever get to know him? His kids?

"You can have dinner with him, Eduardo," her mother said. "He didn't bother to come to his own father's funeral. He wants something from me now?

"Go, Gloria, get your brother. I'm not sharing a meal with this man."

Gloria found Jimmy and Silvia engrossed in the movie. The room flickered and glowed. The girl in the Amazon jungle carefully removed a slippery leech from her skin.

"Come on," Gloria said. "We've got to leave."

Silvia looked up at her. "What?"

"Mama wants to go."

Jimmy pulled his eyes from the TV. "We just got here. The girl's not out of the jungle yet."

"I know it. But she wants to go. Come on."

Gloria trudged toward the hall and heard Silvia and Jimmy slide off the bed behind her, their feet slapping the floor. "Maybe I won't have to play the piano now," Silvia said.

The adults were huddled in a circle by the front door. Her uncle was pressing her mother to stay. The man in the chair stared at his hands, folded on his lap.

"Tell her not to go," her aunt said to her father. Her mother looked determined to leave, despite the persuasion gathering around her.

"Are we leaving?" Jimmy stomped up to her mother in his bare feet, holding his shoes. "But the girl hasn't got out of the jungle yet. Silvia hasn't played the piano. I'm hungry." Her mother urged Jimmy to be quiet.

"Put your shoes on."

"But are we really going?" Her father picked up Jimmy, and he squealed.

"Come on."

Her mother touched the back of Gloria's head when she gave her aunt and uncle a kiss goodbye. "I'm sorry," Dolores said over my head to the man in the chair. "Papa didn't leave me any papers." He looked up at her. "You can probably get a copy of your birth certificate from Mexico," she said, moving out the door.

⌘ ⌘ ⌘

In the car, her mother faced the window as the landscape changed from concrete siding to golden hills threading themselves through the blue sky. The sun was setting, the car filled with rosy light. Her parents were quiet and spent, and her mother's sadness filled the car. Jimmy was now asleep in his seat, slumped low, mouth open. McDonald's wrappers were strewn around their feet below.

When Gloria finally saw the sign on the freeway for their exit, she felt her mother's gaze. "You all right?" she said quietly.

She looked tired and worried, her eyes searching her daughter's face for signs of confusion.

"Will we see him again?"

"What did he say to you?" she asked coldly, as if he were a stranger Gloria shouldn't take candy from.

"He asked me if I'd been to Disneyland."

She blew air out of her mouth and rolled her eyes. "Is that all he had to say? *Dios mío, pendejo.*"

Gloria understood a few words of her mother's tongue, the language lost in her American father's household. "I told him we had."

Her mother turned toward the window again and rubbed her forehead.

"Why did he come?" Gloria asked.

"His birth certificate," she said. "He needs it for something, but I don't have it. Let him find it. That's all he wants."

Their car left the freeway, and they traveled down the long boulevard toward their home. Gloria looked at her family sitting around her in the car, and they suddenly felt precious and important. She looked at each one of them and imagined them as strangers. It felt confusing for a moment to wonder how this man at the wheel, who had grown up far away in South Dakota, had found his way here to California to meet and marry this Latina woman sitting in front of her. Their random arrangement seemed strangely fragile, as if the thing that bound them to one another was just a moment of chance. She called the kid in the back seat her brother. She knew she would call him this for the rest of her life. Her father turned the wheel, and Jimmy stirred from his sleep. The familiar gold field stretched past her window, and she looked across it with relief.

Blind Date

―――――――――

S he wasn't blind, he thought. She could see quite well. She
told him she liked the looks of his suit. It was his only suit.
High, out-of-fashion pockets. He shouldn't have worn the suit,
he thought. To make light of it, he told her he had worn it to
a job interview but hadn't gotten the job. "Hope I have better
luck with it tonight," he said. Then he wished he hadn't said it,
hoped she didn't think he was trying to be too smooth. "Let me
take your jacket," he said. He bought her a corsage. They sat in a
booth with red Naugahyde seats next to a large Mexican family,
and he drank two whole glasses of water before ordering dinner.

It had been two months since his breakup with Jean. Jean was
the woman he had dated for seven long months and had been
set to marry in June. His parents knew Jean. She rode horses and
wore her hair in a bob. Her father owned an electric company
and a house on a hill, trimmed with white lights.

But then he'd met Evelyn, a woman his family knew nothing
about. He really loved Evelyn. At dusk, they'd take tranquil walks
beneath the oak trees. She worked for a Montessori school as a
teacher's aide, and sometimes he'd watch her on the playground

with the children. She'd push them on the swing set or help them make little castles in the sandbox and she was so gentle and soft that he really wanted to put a ring on her finger, but he didn't know how he could and he didn't know how he could take her home to meet his family and she began to wonder why and he didn't know what to tell her, so finally she moved away from him and he never saw her again.

He had been thinking about Evelyn a lot since his breakup with Jean. It got so bad that he couldn't keep his mind on his work. He started to make mistakes and finally sent a shipment of orthopedic shoes to the wrong country. His boss was so angry that he yanked the telephone cord out of the wall and threw a stack of shipment orders into the air like confetti.

He put his head down on his desk until five o'clock came around. Then a coworker, who'd never said more than hello before, set him up on this blind date.

The Mexican family sat around two tables brought together by the window. His date's back faced them, but he could see them, laughing and joking with one another in Spanish. The little round-faced kid at the table had just learned how to say "fuck you," and while the mother tried to quiet him, the group's laughter encouraged him to say it again and again. The old man at the end of the table thought it was funny too, and he kept saying to the kid, "¿Qué dice?" and the kid repeated it.

The family members, he thought, were so comfortable with one another, and he wondered how they had gotten to be that way. As he thought about it, he began to realize how uncomfortable he was. He loosened his tie and stared out the far window. He wasn't thinking about his blind date, or Jean, or even Evelyn. He was thinking about the letter he had received yesterday from his mother. She wanted him to come home for Christmas. She wanted him to bring Jean.

He hadn't told his parents about his breakup with Jean. They thought he was still engaged to her, and he knew they were planning an elaborate spread for Christmas dinner, one they couldn't afford, but it wouldn't matter. His mother would still have the best champagne on the table for Jean.

"What do your parents do?" she asked. His blind date asked the question.

"They're caretakers," he said, looking her straight in the eyes.

What he didn't say was that he used to come home from school on the bus with the rest of the kids and the bus stopped in front of the Grummer estate. That was on Long Island. His parents lived in Salt Lake City now. But the bus would stop and he would get off and pretend that the big house was his. It had ivy climbing up its brick chimney and a long driveway that curved around to the other side. He'd walk up the drive as if the house in front were his, rather than the small cottage in back. Sometimes he'd even check the mailbox.

You do those things when you're a kid, he thought. Had his date done those things when she was a kid? he wondered. And why *had* he done that when he was a kid? Everybody on the bus knew he was the caretaker's son.

She reached for her glass of wine. The base of the glass knocked the corsage he had bought her. It had three small yellow roses tied with a lace bow. She hadn't been able to pin it to stay on her dress, so she had carried it with her to the restaurant. It rested on the table, next to the bread plate.

Her eyes studied him for a while. He wanted to think of something to say, but the only thing that came to mind was paper lunch sacks. So he said, "Paper lunch sacks. Did you have the kind that came in packs of a hundred?"

"When?" she said.

"When you were a kid."

She didn't say anything, but she looked for the waiter. He decided to continue.

"We fought over the paper lunch sacks," he said, "my brothers and I. I was the oldest, but it didn't matter. My parents made us use the ones they brought home from the grocery store. You know, the big ones with 'Safeway' or 'King Kullen' printed on them in red letters?"

"Oh, paper lunch sacks," she said. So he continued.

"All the kids had the small ones that came in packs of a hundred. Once in a while, Mom came home with a small bag from the pharmacy where she picked up Kaopectate to calm the nerves in her stomach. We'd fight for the small bag the whole way to school."

"Sounds like an early disturbance of ego boundaries," she said.

"A what?" he said.

"I read it in a psychology book."

Suddenly, he could feel his glasses on his face. He'd never felt aware of the glasses on his face when he wore them. He knew he wasn't supposed to feel them; they were an extension of his eyes. But now they slumped like two heavy sacks on the bridge of his nose. For a moment, he thought they might crush his nose and he would bleed all over the white tablecloth. With his left hand, he pushed his glasses back. He slid his finger down the top of his nose to make sure it still held together. "¿Qué dice? ¿Qué dice?" he heard the old man say to the kid. The mother suppressed a smile as she grabbed the kid around the waist to prevent him from leaping off the chair.

He looked at his date, and she was watching him. "Are you uncomfortable?" she asked.

"No," he said, bringing his finger down from his nose.

"Good," she said. "I think openness is a positive thing."

"I do too. More wine?" he said, wiping his palms on his knees beneath the tablecloth.

❊ ❊ ❊

Just before nine o'clock, they finished dinner. The Mexican family had left, and the busboy still hadn't cleaned their table. It was a battlefield: white napkins on the floor, rice splattered across the tabletop, glasses downed like tired soldiers. A jazz band started to play a lazy tune in the lounge.

He paid the bill and waited near the front entrance for his blind date to come out of the bathroom. It crossed his mind that she might never emerge. She might have climbed through the bathroom window and called a cab. He thought about driving home alone, and the idea was almost comforting, but then she came out of the bathroom door with freshly applied lipstick.

"I need some air," she said.

They walked along the bike path that followed the coastline. He told her it was the first thing he liked about California: there were bike paths everywhere.

He had his hands in his pockets, and he buttoned his coat. The fog was rolling in and blanketing the stars. The corsage hung upside down in her hand, and he could hear the sound of loose sand crackling beneath the soles of her espadrilles.

He thought about his mother's letter again, and he wondered if he should get back together with Jean before the holidays.

"How long have you lived in California?" she asked.

"Two years," he said. "It's the longest I've lived anywhere in my life."

They walked by an old man in tattered clothes with a pack hanging from his shoulder. He was bent over, talking to a scrawny dog by a water fountain. The man lifted the dog's front paws gently and rested them on the rim of the fountain. He watched the man turn on the water so the dog could take a drink, and he thought of Evelyn making little sandcastles with the children.

"My father liked to move around a lot," he said.

In fact, he wanted to say, *I've seen the entire country through my father's failures. Boise, Long Island, Des Moines, Charlotte, Pensacola, Fort Collins . . .*

"Fort Collins," he said. "Now, there's a town I'll never return to. My father bought a deli in Fort Collins. He always had a new get-rich-quick scheme. Stinking sauerkraut and liverwurst. The whole family helped him run it. I used to stand next to my little brother near the washbasin in the back room and pour mayonnaise into tiny plastic cups."

They came to a bench facing the ocean and sat down. He could hear the waves rolling on the beach, but he couldn't see the horizon because the ocean matched the dark color of the sky.

"Do you carry a lot of anger toward your father?" she asked.

"I felt responsible for that deli," he said. "While my brothers were out playing, I stayed inside and did another tray of mayonnaise. I'd stay an extra hour and slice the pickles."

What he didn't say was that the mayonnaise spoiled because nobody came to eat at the deli, and that his father lost what they'd saved in a pyramid scheme. His parents started to argue—another failed business venture, and they had nothing to show for it.

"It has something to do with being the firstborn," she said. "The oldest child feels responsible for fixing the family while the other kids play."

"Firstborn-itis," he said. *She should know*, he thought. *She read those books.*

He closed his eyes for a moment and felt the cool air on his cheeks. He remembered sitting on the steps inside the deli when his father was forced to put it up for sale. His shirt was splattered with mayonnaise, and his eyelids were squeezed shut because he was wishing hard for someone to come and save them. "Please, God," he said on those steps, "make someone come in and buy this stinking deli."

He opened his eyes. He watched her stare toward the ocean, her eyelashes catching the fog. They sat quietly for a moment, until a strong breeze whipped sand against their ankles. They both stood.

"I would take you dancing," he said, "but I didn't wear my dancing shoes." He said this to be funny, but she didn't laugh.

The corsage slid across the dashboard when he turned the corner toward her house. "It's coming up on the right," she said. He slowed the car and pulled up alongside the curb. "It wasn't so bad," she said, "for a blind date, but do you mind if I don't kiss you?"

He looked at her through his clear, round glasses. "No," he said. "Do you mind if I don't call you again?"

They both laughed, and little bursts of steam leapt from their mouths into the cold air. He wanted to say there was just one more thing. *I dated this woman named Jean for seven miserable months, even though I didn't like her. She had lots of money, her family was rich, and my mother wished for me to marry her. What do you think about that? What do those books say about that?*

"Take care," he said.

"Yeah," she said. "Have a good life." And she got out of the car.

He watched her walk to the front door, turn the key. Light filled the doorway, and then the door shut. He turned the key to his ignition and pitched the steering wheel to the left. The corsage bounced off the dash and fell to the floor.

❀ ❀ ❀

When he arrived home, he sat in the corner desk in the room he rented. He was comfortable sitting alone in his stiff wood chair, facing a blank wall. The phone still rested on the table in the hallway, and he thought about picking it up to call Evelyn.

"Hello, Evelyn," he rehearsed. "I haven't seen you in a while."

He rolled his eyes. He still had on his only suit, even the jacket. He wondered what it would be like to sleep in a suit, to let it wrinkle and lose shape without worry. But before he tried it, he pulled a piece of paper from the top desk drawer.

"Dear Evelyn," he wrote, stopping to shake his pen because the ink had run dry. His cuff links shook. "I've been thinking about you a lot. Did I ever tell you that I had firstborn-itis, and perhaps a host of other maladies that stem from my careful pouring of mayonnaise into tiny plastic cups?"

He put the pen down and walked to the calendar tacked to the back of his bedroom door. He flipped through pictures of America's national parks to the month of December. He counted the weeks until Christmas. He thought of his mother, Santa Claus, candied yams, and paper lunch sacks. Then he let the pages of the calendar fall and swing from the anchor of their thumbtack.

He crumpled the letter and drew another piece of paper from the desk. "Dear Evelyn," he wrote, "Dear Evelyn." He sat back on his bed with the letter and pen. He didn't stop to remove his suit. He only loosened the knot of his paisley-print tie.

Staircase Interlude

She sits at a table in a Greek restaurant, and it occurs to her that there is a staircase in the room.

It is not an unusual staircase, although the light coming through the window of the front door illuminates it brightly. She wonders why she has never seen anyone climb its steps. She doesn't know where it leads, what is on the second floor.

She decides to imagine a story about the staircase because she is tired of watching the front door, because she is through rearranging her hands on the table. She knows what she wants for lunch and will not reread the selections in the menu again; there is time to kill, her friend usually fifteen minutes late.

She begins with a description of the staircase. It is a good place to start, her eyes relieved of the front door. The staircase is made of handsome pinewood planks. Each step is polished, a deep sheen on either side of worn centers—oblong circles, she thinks, from days of use, sturdy soles, and lost grace.

The light cuts across the steps, clear and pure, so vivid it resembles the Mediterranean light of the Old World. It gives the staircase an appearance outside time, she notices. It could be the only staircase, the one all others imitate.

❊ ❊ ❊

A waiter refills her water glass. He wears a sleeveless sweater vest, buttoned. He walks with a bend in his knees, the supports of his tall frame weakening. The ice cubes rattle in her glass. He smiles down at her compassionately.

Half of the hour passes. Shadows cross the balustrade and steps. She knows there are stories within the shadows, stories within her story, told over and over again. At one thirty, her friend thirty minutes late, the shadow is the story of a black anvil, the sixth and seventh steps erased in its dark triangle; at five o'clock, she imagines, it will be the tale of a mimosa, its leaves weightless and diffuse. The mimosa will blend into full shadow, and then a small ceiling lamp will faintly light the staircase. Once the natural light is gone, the polish, the grooves, and the lines will blur.

She can sense the staircase breathing and swallowing, its wood absorbing the scents from the kitchen, the honey-sweet baklava, the pungent feta.

Her mind drifts across the staircase. She sees pictures of the staircase's travelers, climbing the steps. Though she cannot describe the faces of these characters, she sees their legs. Passing are bent knees in twill trousers, thick leather shoes pulling slowly beneath pant legs.

The legs pass a backdrop of white brick. The bricks in the wall are thickly formed, pitted, heavy with paint. A travel poster of Ios hangs loosely on the wall. It is a view through a whitewashed windowsill of the Aegean Sea, undulating degrees of blue green. The steps form a jagged line beneath the poster like a strong current; the passing legs ride its tug and release.

She thinks of Greece, imagining the second floor as an alcove of the Old World. The legs belong to Greek immigrants, she decides, who come to gather in a place of their own. Stories leave the shadows and take the form of words. She writes them on the paper mat beneath her fork and spoon. In scrawling No. 2 lead, they sing *rebetika* of loneliness: "The moon is down / The darkness is deep / Only one man / Cannot fall asleep." They play backgammon for unusable drachmas and toast with pale green glasses of retsina. Dimming light tints the room a soft shade of blue.

A Greek man rests an elbow on a wobbly table. She can picture him on the second floor with his cronies. A former sponge diver, he speaks of the bends. His porous hands move in the air as he talks. He tells of Kalymnos, complains about the New World news. He remembers tenderizing octopus against a stone ledge. Flat roofs and terraces. The Italian occupation. The island of Ios, he argues, is the real birthplace of Homer.

The ice cubes float, diminished, in her glass. At fifty minutes late, she reminds herself never to meet this friend at a restaurant. She orders a glass of retsina and toasts to a bad idea.

How long will she sit, she wonders, without lunch with a friend fifty-five minutes late? The waiter refills her water glass, and, like a bum without a place to go, she decides to stay a little longer.

Not too much longer. The sign in the window reads *Closing at 10:00 p.m.*, and though she knows it is hours before closing, it is a gentle reminder that she is taking up space, possibly dinner space if she does not order lunch.

So she imagines how her characters will leave the restaurant, hoping it will make it easier for her.

They descend the staircase together, down the cliff-hung steps to the winding streets below. She can feel the ride; the staircase bears its travelers like a mule. Their legs scrape the walls, and they're fearful of a stumble. They line the white brick—the sponge diver, the twill trousers, and she—cats in the cupolas of a former world.

The staircase breathes and swallows; the stair light flickers and drowns.

And an empty chair sits far from the table, its guest having left in a hurry. A crumpled napkin, melted ice. She has left more dollars on the table than necessary, marking a time when waiting for someone was an imaginative art, long before the convenience of the cell phone.

Engaged

They came around the corner in Gary's red Camaro, the last stretch of road between them and the yellow one-story with its two front windows like great, giant eyes, blinking and watching. It was hot out this evening. They rolled all the windows down so strong gusts of dry, Indian summer air whipped around them. She was slouched in her seat, arms outstretched through the window, playing with the rushing wind and watching the way her new ring gleamed and changed colors with the sunset.

Gary didn't speak, and she was content with a little silence. Their lips were swollen red, and her jaw ached from all the kissing. They were returning from their secret spot, the place hidden from the crooked road that led to the lake. They had laid a blanket there, behind his Camaro, and groped for each other like stranded castaways beside the mustard plants and the rusty water tank someone had discarded.

Afterward, he had bent down on one knee. He lost his balance when he reached into his pocket for the velvet box. But she stood as still as the lake over the ridge, her eyes passing through Gary's, through the back of his skull, down the crooked road, to the last stretch where the one-story sat, a yellow marker in a town too small to locate on a map.

Gary's Camaro whisked by each telephone pole, one after the other, drawing them nearer, teasing them along the way. Her skin flushed, and heat rose to her eyes. The straight road left dust behind them.

"Would you quit that?" he said, glancing at her arm fluttering out the window. "It makes me nervous."

She drew her arm in. She saw the look of concentration on his face, as if he were rehearsing in his mind, over and over. He tried to look relaxed. He tapped his finger against the steering wheel in time with the music, his high school ring tight around his swollen, clammy finger. One arm rested on the door; his legs were spread apart, faded blue jeans stretched over his knees. She noticed his new haircut. The brown waves that used to touch his collar and cover his ears were gone. His hair lay in straight, clean lines, outlining his ears now, showing his collar rubbing the fresh stubble on the back of his neck.

She stared at Gary as her father would. She tried to become her dad, slouched in her seat, examining Gary from outside herself, from far away, atop a perch inside her father's mind.

Young, maybe, she thought, but he had a good job.

Gary worked full-time at Rancho Hardware, a store with a twenty-five-year history in the town's first row of shops. In another year, his job wouldn't matter anymore. They would pack their things and leave the town. But it mattered now.

They passed a row of eucalyptus trees, and the sweet, mint-green odor filled her nose. The Camaro swept by the sagging bark, loose and flapping in the dry wind.

"Think he's in a good mood?" Gary asked.

"Good as any," she said, straightening her blouse.

Gary had been the only boy in high school who acted like

he didn't belong in the town. She could remember the exact day she had felt this about him. He'd hung by his hands from the second-floor balcony at school, and their old, fuzzy math teacher ran in a panic for help. He hoisted himself back onto the balcony before the teacher returned, and she watched him swagger down the hall to his next class.

On their first date, his blue jeans brushed against her skirt and the touch made her feel stark naked. Then, when their senior year rushed to a close, she told him his touch was a drink of cold water chasing a burn down her throat. His eyes grew wide. They fell onto the cold, tiled floor of his parents' bathroom before she knew it. Gary flushed the toilet several times so nobody could hear them.

He pulled the car into the drive. The family-room window was open, and she could hear the TV. A sports announcer's voice hovered just above a whisper, then hushed for a pin drop, followed by a burst of applause. She knew her dad was watching golf.

"Better not park here," she said. "Your car leaks oil on the drive."

"I fixed that."

She sat in the car, staring at the house. She knew when her father disliked a guy. She would bring a date in to meet him, and he could sum him up without batting an eye, without missing a beat. *No, Dad*, she could hear herself saying, *you've got it all wrong. I'm eighteen and old enough to know this is the one.*

"You got cold feet?" Gary asked, standing outside the car, his head poking through her window.

"I don't know," she said. "I was just thinking that the house looked different."

He leaned against the car door and stared at the house, pretending to study it. "How so?"

"Do you ever feel like you've outgrown things?"

He pulled open her door. "Only my pants," he said, grinning. "Come on. Let's get going."

She slid out slowly. She wondered how the house would change itself into somebody else's house, somebody who planned to spend more time with it when she was gone.

✕ ✕ ✕

Her father sat in his worn recliner. They said their hellos and sat down on the couch to wait for the commercial, as if they had nothing important to say. They might discuss the weather or a new store that had opened. Gary kept shifting on the couch, changing the way he placed his legs. She sunk her left hand down beside her thigh to hide its shiny message.

At her age, she thought, giving herself courage, her father had married a girl he had known for only two weeks! He had never told her that part of the story; she had discovered it herself. What she'd learned came from the bottom of his sock drawer, where old photographs and a few letters lay hidden. There were pictures of him, young and lean, wearing saddle shoes, sometimes a fedora half-cocked on his head. He'd looked as shiny as a brass knob then, and the woman on his arm was not her mother but a small, pretty, blond woman with a grin as wide as the brim of his hat.

His first marriage ended, a fact that sent him west in search of a new beginning. Her mother was the new beginning for a little over two years, and then she was gone. He didn't tell her much about that either. His past didn't exist for her, and when she saw the photographs, he seemed like a different man, someone she didn't know, and perhaps someone he didn't want her to know.

Gary glanced at her nervously. He sat back and wiped his damp palms across his pant legs. Her dad looked tired, a night's wrestle with insomnia showing in puffs above his pale cheeks. He wore a plaid flannel shirt, one of the many he had in different colors. She knew that his drooping eyes were taking everything in: he would know the color of Gary's socks as quickly as he would know the handicap of the guy on the fifth hole.

A commercial for house paint came on the air, and a man in overalls demonstrated how the other brand of paint chipped and faded in the dry weather. Skip, their dog, sat on the floor next to her dad, whose fingertips reached down to stroke the shaggy tan fur.

"What do you know?" His eyes swept past them and returned to the TV. Gary straightened and pulled at the waist of his pants like men do when attention turns to them.

"How's the tournament?" Gary asked, in that deep tone reserved for adults.

"Koepka ahead."

"That's good," Gary said, sliding back in his seat again and pulling his jeans down at the knees. "Mr. Garrett, " he said, as if rehearsing for a broadcasting role, "Dana and I've got something important to tell you."

Her father turned his attention to them slowly. Skip spread out on the carpet and rolled over. He wiggled that way, his paws in the air, itching a place on his back.

"Dana and I decided to get married this afternoon. I mean, I gave her the ring this afternoon." He grabbed her right hand for evidence without thinking. She lifted her left hand and raised the ring finger.

"Very nice," he said.

"We thought about it for a while," Gary said.

"All of senior year," Dad said, a little dryly.

The tournament came back on, and the hushed drone of the announcer filled the quiet room. The sound made her think of lawn mowers working on a hot summer day, the buzz floating in waves to the backyard, where she'd doze on the warm ground.

He reached over and turned off the TV. She suddenly wondered if she was really doing this, sitting on the couch like an outsider in her own life. She wanted someone to tell her what was happening, tell her she was doing the wrong thing so she could tell that person that she could make up her own mind.

"Dad," she heard herself saying, "we'd like to marry in the backyard."

He sat back on his recliner and looked out the window. A kid rode by on a bicycle, his sun-bleached hair hanging over his eyes. "So you two are in love?" he asked, turning to them, his face outlined by the window.

She thought he looked calm, only like he was choosing to be calm, rather than feeling it, as if he had picked one way to be over another.

"We're in love, Dad."

"In love, are you?"

His mouth angled forward at the jaw, drawing his lips upward. She knew this expression because she used it too. She used it when she concentrated, and it made her look serious, as she often did in photographs, unlike her mother in that snapshot taken at a Las Vegas chapel.

"How do you plan to support each other?"

"I've got a good job," Gary said. "I'll probably be assistant manager by the end of the year."

Gary grinned at her, and she looked at him again, as if from a distance. She saw him small and flawed in her house, where her dad sat in his recliner next to the window where she often dreamed about the outside world. She wanted Gary to go back in his truck to the gold field by the lake, where he loomed larger than life in the small town and she didn't second-guess her decision.

Her dad watched them, the empty black TV screen beside him, more noticeable off than on.

"You two say you're in love," he said with a long sigh. "As much as two people can be at eighteen, I guess. Isn't that right, Dana? Gary? You two know what it's like to be married at eighteen?"

"No, Dad," she said, Gary putting his arm around her, sending that chill down her backbone. "Did you?"

⁂

They joined her father on the patio for champagne. Dusk settled in, and the air stopped rippling with heat and rested softly at a temperature that blended with their skin.

They lifted their glasses. Skip rolled around on the grass, which grew tall and dry and couldn't be kept green for very long during the summer. The old oak tree bent its back to the sun, its dark, gnarled bark groping for the fallen acorns on the ground.

Her dad made a toast. He said something about embarking on their young lives together, something about trials and tribulations. She wasn't listening carefully. She felt odd toasting with her dad, as if she would need to show ID to prove she was an adult, but nobody asked, so maybe she'd slide by this time. Gary looked clumsy holding the glass of champagne. He stood with his feet crossed and one arm tucked under the other. She felt awkward too, only she felt better able to pretend that she didn't, and looking at her dad she wondered if that was the key, that being an adult was just getting better at pretending, better at it with practice, making champagne toasts dozens of times.

⁂

Back in Gary's car, they drove past the telephone poles in the opposite direction, dark outside, a few lights in the distance making little halos against the slate sky. Gary held her hand and drove with the other. He pressed his foot down hard on the accelerator and stuck his head out the window a few times so the wind messed his hair.

"You got your hair cut for my dad, didn't you?" she asked.

"No," he said, in a high tone that told her he was lying. "It just needed to be cut. But I can't stand the way that lady styles it."

They drove toward his parents' house. Gary seemed relaxed and loose, now that the tension was gone, but his adrenaline was still pumping.

"It went good with your father, don't you think?" He turned the corner sharply, the tires screeching.

"I think so."

"Your dad's all right. I thought he'd say, 'You're too young to get married.' But he didn't. He was cool."

He made a turn that took them in the wrong direction, up a steep dirt road that led to the top of a hill overlooking the small town, still and vacant, and the dark patch where their high school sat. Lining the road were cacti, boulders, and tumbleweeds. Gary rolled up his window to stop dust from blowing into the car.

"Where are we going?" she asked.

"I thought we'd take a look at the view," he said, grinning.

She tossed his hand away playfully. The car curved around a bend and rose to the top of the hill, where she could no longer see the road or walls carved out of the rocky hillside, only sky, endless evening sky, and nothing of the town below. The car came to a stop. She saw its hood extending out, as if suspended in air. She felt as if the car's tires could leave the scarred, bumpy dirt and sail away.

The seat was cramped and her knees were up, Gary's head hitting the roof. Outside it was quiet. A gentle breeze swept loose dirt against the side of the car, and she heard a lone coyote cry. *If we could just stay like this*, she thought, *on the hilltop with the coyote, above the town below.* Her mind would be quiet then; it would just quit talking.

"Gary," she said, "when will we go away? Why don't we just pick anywhere on a map and go?"

Gary looked at her, his eyes trying to focus, as if they'd been rolled up inside his head. "We can't leave," he said.

"What do you mean?" she said. "Why can't we?"

He brought his fingers to her lips. "I've got a good job here. Besides, what about our friends? Why do you want to leave?"

He kissed her on the mouth. The windows fogged over, and she couldn't see outside anymore. She felt her dreams slipping away, but she didn't know how to catch them. A soft glow shone through the back window, murky and hazy, like the small, haloed lights in the distance, only this was the moon.

T-Zone

That he should come to his sister's house, to see her, who had married the perfect man, the man who had never muddled an opportunity in his life or second-guessed himself, revealed how desperate he was for some true punishment.

Be flown to San Francisco, he told himself, take a bus to her place, be greeted by Anita and his flawless brother-in-law. What would they see? First, his shaved head. The immediate humiliation of cadet hazing week. Then his scuffed leather shoes and jeans frayed at the hems, symbols of his inner resistance to the spit-shine mythology. And his walk, a little hesitant and light. He couldn't shake it, no matter how hard he tried. He felt like the dog-eared page of a paperback.

From the thinly paved road, he looked at his sister's house. A white clapboard from the early 1930s, on its way to matching the restored elegance of the other homes on the block. The maroon BMW parked in the drive.

His brother-in-law, Carl, with a full head of dark, curly hair, clean chinos and T-shirt, and the carriage of a man used to landing squarely on his feet, greeted him at the door.

"Russell, you're here!" Carl took the duffel bag from his shoulder as if he'd been expecting him. Not "What are you doing here?" or "What happened to you?" Russell felt slightly disappointed.

"I'm out, Carl. A medical discharge."

"Well . . ." Carl let it trail off like an unanswerable question. Did he mean, *Such is life*? Russell wondered. Or, *This is what we expected of you*?

"I'll put your bag in the guest room." Carl motioned to the back of the house with his head. "Come out to the porch once you're settled. Help me put this kite together."

He was a man, Russell thought, who had a prescription for everything. When his sister couldn't decide whether she wanted to marry him, he left for a ten-day bike ride, and when he returned she begged him for the ring.

Russell secretly envied that confidence. His father called Carl "a real go-getter," with an implied nudge to pay attention thrown Russell's way. "Carl the Go-Kart," Russell had liked to tease his sister, and she had had the sportiveness then—Russell would give her that—to laugh along with him.

Russell's deepest suspicion: that his father would prefer someone like Carl for a son. Hadn't Russell watched his father ride Carl's successes with the joy of a man vindicating his own lost dreams? The pats on the back? Celebration dinners that Carl rushed to pay for with his American Express?

It had not been easy growing up with his father. He had been, in his mythical former life, during the Korean War—before children and a mortgage, before cancer took his wife away—a drill sergeant for the Marines. He now read gas meters for the Edison Company in suburban neighborhoods lined with fences.

"You expect too much," he told Russell when he left his job as a fact-checker for a current-events magazine. Other jobs followed—most loosely tied to his all-purpose political science degree. "In my day," his father liked to say, "there was no time to dawdle."

Carl dropped his bag on the floor of the guest room. "Where's Anita?" Russell asked.

"She just got home from work," he called over his shoulder. "She's making a phone call."

His sister was director of something to do with new accounts at a bank. Russell had seen her title once, printed beneath her name on a bronze plate. He couldn't remember exactly what it said, but every desk had one and they seemed to declare not only territories but reasons for being as well. Russell remembered thinking how reassuring those declarations must be: *This is where I sit. This is what I am.*

Alone in the guest room, Russell noticed it had been redecorated in cream-colored fabric, which reminded him of a starched, impeccably folded restaurant napkin. He felt the urge to mess up the bedcover, to throw himself on it and thrash around.

"I thought once you signed up, they never let you out."

At the sound of the familiar voice, Russell turned to face his sister, Anita, who stood in the doorway. Her freckles had blurred bronze on her still-childlike cheeks, but the alteration stopped him short. It was less the business suit and heels than the full-force expression on her face, the erasure of daydreams, the indistractability. She seemed to know exactly what she wanted.

"I parked my jet on the roof," he said. "Hope it's not a problem."

Did she remember how they used to talk? Russell wondered. She slumped onto an upholstered chair and flipped her shoes off. "My feet are killing me," she said, rubbing one. "Does Dad know?"

"Not yet."

"You're not AWOL, are you?"

"Of course not. I was NPQ'd," he said, appreciating for the first time one of the Navy's never-ending supply of acronyms, softening its impact before he had to translate.

She looked up from her foot. "What's that?"

"Not physically qualified." Was there ever a more humbling term? The Naval Aerospace Medical Institute doctor, or NAMI Nazi, as the flight candidates liked to call him, had discovered the slight curve in his spine. And Russell had felt then (hadn't he?) a great rush of relief.

"Oh," she said. Her voice dropped.

"I've got curvature of the spine."

She rolled her eyes. "How'd you get that?"

"I don't know," he said. "Probably from all those years of being told to sit up straight. It disqualified me from the flight program. They sent me home."

"Well, I couldn't see you as a pilot anyway," she said.

"Really?"

"No. I always pictured you as something else. Not a pilot." She pulled her feet up onto the chair and crossed them under her. Russell wished she would tell him what she pictured him as, but he didn't have the courage to ask. When he had come upon the idea of becoming a fighter pilot, something in him had been triggered and crystallized—as he combed through the paperwork and waited for his acceptance—into a stainless-steel direction. For now, he wouldn't dream of unraveling the origins of that choice. Yet there it had been in front of him, the career he was meant to have.

"I'd like to stay a little while," Russell said, wondering if she guessed it was a trial run before he owned up to his failure in front of his father.

She shot him a look, both maternal and provoking. Big sister. "Do you have anywhere else better to go?"

✄ ✄ ✄

Later, stepping out of the shower, Russell stole a glance at himself in the mirror, his face a composite of angles without his hair. The first real look he'd had since it had been shaved off, and it confirmed his worst suspicion: his head was definitely flatter on the left side.

T-Zone: the murky place Russell had floated in for a month, waiting for the Navy's final word on his discharge. Somewhere like purgatory, a noncommittal place for those candidates not ready "to go up." He waited there in his "uniform of the day," khakis, most often, which felt sticky and hot in the Florida gulf air.

Once, while delivering a package to a lieutenant, he'd watched the flight candidates tread water in full flight gear with helmets. Forty minutes later, they were still there, struggling not to sink in the pool like ceramic pots. *What am I doing here?* he'd wondered. *What did I think I would prove?*

Now, in fresh civilian clothes, he found Carl working on the glassed-in back porch. Through the window he saw their well-tended yard, the garden that seemed enviably copied from a *House Beautiful* magazine.

He scanned the worktable, arranged with nylon sheets, tubing, plastic clips, white line, a book on the history of kites, and another on kite construction. Next to him was an orange-colored sheet. Carl held up a triangle of purple nylon, then flipped it over, the frame like a spine raised against smooth skin. Russell watched him handle the frame. His hands were boxy and muscular, tanned, with some dark hairs along the edge. His fingers moved nimbly, gently, along the connections, and Russell felt a stirring inside him that seemed familiar, though he couldn't place it.

Russell shifted his gaze to the diagrams on the table, complicated instructions that created a delta-shaped stunt kite. It *would* be this kite, he thought. Not a simple flat kite with a tail.

He sat down on an uncomfortable wicker chair and thumbed through Carl's kite history book, through the facts, dates, and illustrations. "When did you start flying kites?"

"A couple months ago," Carl said, clipping white line onto the frame. "There's a group that gets together at Golden State Park."

He was this kind of man, Russell thought. Picking hobbies like numbers out of a hat—biking, mountain climbing, windsurfing—and instantly becoming expert at them, with the carefree easiness of a California dream boy. He remembered when he and Carl had played badminton in his father's backyard a week before his sister's marriage. His father, still dressed in his SoCal Edison uniform, had played referee. He'd sat slouched in a redwood chair, a Coors beer hanging from his hand. "That's out, Russ!" he'd called.

Anita, still in her bikini, sat restlessly, pretending to be more interested in the sun beating down on her body than in the game. Every ten minutes or so, she rose to get something from the kitchen like a disgusted cheerleader. *When will you two give it up?* her body language shouted.

Russell would not give it up. His father's calls flushed his face red. "Too long, Russ!" or, "Didn't you see that shot coming?" Russell remembered an unusual charge running through him. He was not willing to give up the game; he had needed to keep Carl on the other side of the net.

"I'm finishing this for the festival," Carl said. "It's a stunt kite. Let's try it out later."

Russell opened the book to a random page. "What year did Benjamin Franklin fly his kite in the thunderstorm?" Russell quizzed.

"Seventeen fifties?"

"Fifty-two. When did the National Weather Service stop using box kites to predict weather?"

Carl scowled.

"You should know," Russell said. "You're making a kite. Nineteen thirty-three."

"Hmm. That late?"

Russell remembered the naval doctor's deciding question: "Do you experience back pain?"

"Sometimes," Russell had said, lying. He'd never had a back cramp in his life. Yet the X-rays had shown it. It had really been there.

But it felt peculiar to have the decision made for him by something beyond his control. Somehow he felt as if his own indecision had had a hand in it. "Mind over matter," his father would have said. For now, he was just able to sit with this new confusion, to feel its blurred outline before attempting to fill it in.

"Do you know the Old English word for 'kite'?" Carl asked.

Russell looked up from his book—*Damn him,* he thought, *still attractive when being a nerd*—then slammed it shut.

The sun was beginning to set, and a pink, dusky glow settled on the roofs of houses.

"*Kait,*" Carl said. "A predatory bird."

⌘ ⌘ ⌘

Russell and Carl roamed the supermarket's fluorescent aisles, the squeaky cart rolling past familiar brand names—Kellogg's, General Foods, Stouffer's, Nabisco—that restored in Russell a sense of equilibrium. If one ever needed neutral territory, the supermarket was the place to visit. No confusion here. The land of the brand name was everybody's home.

In the cart was a box of Uncle Ben's rice. Carl had added bottled water and white wine. Russell had offered to cook dinner tonight. He had one standard meal he could cook when he needed to: boxed rice, steak, salad with a few tomatoes and croutons tossed on top. The two guys were giving Anita a much-needed break to go to the gym.

Russell pushed the jerky cart over to the meat section, a blast of refrigerated air skidding across his scalp. A woman piled packaged chicken breasts one on top of the other, searching for something Russell suspected she wouldn't find. He grabbed a T-bone steak.

"You know Anita's a vegetarian, don't you?"

"When did that happen?" Russell asked.

"For about a year now," Carl said. "She says she's got more energy."

"You're a vegetarian too?"

"Have been," Carl laughed. "Don't you remember the vegetarian dishes I made for the wedding?" Russell tossed the T-bone back into the refrigerated bin. "That drove your father crazy," he said.

He pushed the cart down another aisle, unaware of its contents. He was bothered by Anita's attention to the little details of her life while he struggled with the larger plan. He looked up for the sign: PASTA, LEGUMES, SOUPS, SAUCES. He floated up and down the aisles, a shipwrecked sailor searching for home, until he finally conceded that he had no idea what to cook.

"I've got the perfect thing," Carl said. "You like Chinese?"

In the vegetable section, Carl filled the cart with items Russell had never known existed: bok choy, ginger root, bamboo shoots.

When Anita came into the kitchen, showered and changed into comfortable clothes, he and Carl were there together, cooking. It had not started out that way, until Russell conceded that stir-fry was out of his repertoire. While Carl prepared the wok, he instructed Russell to slice vegetables.

"Cut them lengthwise," he said. Russell ignored him.

Carl poured peanut oil into the sizzling wok. Russell caught him eyeing the vegetables he was cutting. "Let me show you," Carl said, reaching from behind him to guide the knife.

Russell felt the strange feeling again; its familiarity bothered him. He jerked away. "What's it matter, Carl? Does it have to be perfect?"

"Well, it cooks differently when—"

"Does it matter if I cut them this way? Who the hell cares?"

Carl drew back. "Take it easy, Russ."

Anita stood up from the kitchen table. "Bro," she said, "let's go for a walk."

He followed Anita out onto the cool night asphalt, and they walked along the road toward the curve where it turned to dirt and led to the potter's bungalow, a low, shingled structure nearly covered with ivy. The air was cool, as nights were in early spring. Russell felt glad for the dryness too, after swallowing steamy gulf air those months in Florida. He still felt uneasily stirred and, not knowing what to do about it, kicked a rock so that it struck a tin trash can and made a satisfying *clang*.

"You're pathetic," Anita said, her voice just audible above the echo.

"*I'm* pathetic." He felt his face flush to his scalp, and he ran a hand over the nubs.

"What did you come here for?" she asked. "So you could measure yourself up to Carl again? What is it with you?"

Frustration rose through him. He had actually missed her. He remembered walking through an empty shopping mall while on leave and being reminded of his sister. It had been the smell of cinnamon. She used to boil cinnamon sticks in a pot during the holidays. Yet now he felt the giant span between them. She didn't understand him at all.

"I'm not measuring myself against . . ." Then he stopped, because he realized that it might be better if she didn't understand him. The five years of mockery, of slant-mouthed derision, of calling Carl "Anita's G.I. Joe," suddenly felt like pathetic attempts to deny his own attraction.

"Just stop." Anita rubbed her forehead with the heels of both hands, and she instantly looked older, more like a woman than a sister. He noticed this for the first time and felt strange that he had missed it along the way. Before Carl and Anita married, Russell had thought his sister would be stifled by Carl's success. Choked and smothered. But he had been wrong. It dawned on him that what he had feared for Anita may have been what he desired for himself.

"I'm sorry, Anita," he said, tossing a pebble at the toe of his shoe. "You're right. I don't know why I came."

She was quiet for a while; then she let out a sigh. She threw her arm up on his shoulder and knocked her hip against him like she used to when they were younger. "You came because you missed me," she said. "Admit it, or I'll put Silly Putty in your shoes."

⚜ ⚜ ⚜

The next morning, Russell lay in bed as the workday routine rumbled outside his door. Smell of coffee. Clink of spoons against ceramic. Shop talk: Who will pick up the laundry, and who will get the fixings for dinner? Then shoes thumped and closet doors squeaked, shower and faucet ran, until he heard the antique door close with a heavy thud and two engines gurgle down the driveway. Silence. He lay in it, still as a cat in headlights. The day stretched before him like one long, somnolent void.

He got up and walked to the kitchen. At the sink, he filled the coffeepot with water and noticed the one bowl left in the basin.

The pool of blue-gray milk at the bottom, a few cornflakes stuck to the sides. He looked for the other bowl and found it: washed, along with the spoon, and set to drip-dry on the wooden dish rack. He knew it was Carl's.

In the refrigerator, he found a slice of pepperoni pizza. He bent it into a funnel and tore a bite off the tip. On the front page of the refolded newspaper was a bright yellow sticky note: "Russ, we should be home a little early tonight. Friday! Do me a favor and go to the hobby shop around the corner for some more line. Dacron rather than nylon if they have it. Trial run tonight. Thanks, Carl." Beneath the note was a twenty-dollar bill.

Russell had no idea what type of line Carl needed, so he decided to lug the entire kite to the store.

Outside, the air was crisp and blue. He walked with the kite fluttering behind him. It gave him a feeling of childhood again, the kite dancing along, like a cape behind his back. When he saw that it might float a little, he let out some more line, but the kite bucked and then drooped, defeated, toward the asphalt.

In the hobby store, he found Pete, the "kite guy" he had been told about at the front counter. Pete was in the back of the shop. He wore khaki shorts with a T-shirt announcing a decathlon that had taken place a year earlier. He was extraordinarily fit, wore his graying hair in a ponytail, and had waxed his handlebar moustache into two firm points.

Russell set Carl's kite on the worktable. He waited to catch the kite man's attention. "I need some line. Dacron. I have no idea what that is, so I brought in the whole kite."

Pete walked over to the table and examined the kite. "Who put this together? You?"

"No. My brother-in-law."

"Well, this kite isn't going up in the air."

Won't go up in the air? Russell almost laughed out loud. "It won't?" He wanted to shake Pete's hand and take him out to lunch.

"No. The bridle setting's all wrong."

"It is?"

"Yeah. You want the turbo setting, and this isn't it. It won't fly the way you want it to. Tell your brother-in-law," he said with a wink, "he needs to recheck it."

Russell picked up the kite as Pete slapped a roll of line onto the counter. He must have mistaken Russell's inward smile for embarrassment. "Aw, hell," he said. "It's my lunch break in five minutes. I'll help you reset it."

"But it's not my—"

"Look," Pete said, pulling some keys out of a drawer, "I'll offer only once. People would stand in line to have me do this. Your brother-in-law, or whoever this is, will have an awesome kite."

⌘ ⌘ ⌘

At a little past six, Russell heard the cars returning from work, then Anita and Carl calling across the street, in conversation with a neighbor. He sat on the porch, looking absently through the kite history book. On the worktable were the repaired kite and the new reel of line.

Running through his mind were the following scenarios: *Carl walks in, and Russell tells him his kite wouldn't have flown if he'd stood beneath it with a high-powered fan. Or Carl walks in, and Russell waits until he notices the different setting, then magnanimously admits to Carl that he's had the kite fixed.* The second scenario pleased him. He replayed it in his head several times before Anita appeared with two greenish tomatoes in her hands. She placed them on the windowsill.

"I won't grow them in my garden. Those gross green worms."

"That's right. Leave them for the good neighbors to grow."

"Yes. Let them deal with the worms." She laughed and flopped down onto the wicker chair. "So, what did you do today?"

"I took a kite for a walk."

"Did it behave?"

"Beautifully."

Carl stepped onto the porch, tossing his sport coat onto a small table. Russell was instantly reminded of Carl's gift for self-possession. He had a way of slipping into and out of roles with some part of his own personality intact. Carl the Silicon Valley whiz. Carl the sportsman, the husband, or whatever. But always Carl. Russell watched him move toward the worktable. In that instant, he felt enormous gratitude for the little bit of knowledge the kite man had given him to share with Carl. Bridle settings. It was too good to be true.

"Thanks for picking up the line," Carl said. "Was it a problem?"

"I don't think so. Unless I got the wrong kind."

Carl casually examined the kite and the new line while Russell stopped breathing, awaiting the perfect moment.

"Great," Carl declared, clapping his hands together. "Let's take her out after dinner, see what she can do."

Russell stared in disappointment. It would have been one thing if Carl had noticed the change and chosen to be silent about it. There would have been a glitch in his examination, a recognition, an understanding, followed by a need to save face. But there was nothing, because he didn't see it. And if he didn't see it, that meant, of course, that only Russell knew.

"Let's go out for dinner," Anita said. "I don't feel like cooking on Friday night."

"Good idea," Carl said. Russell watched him exit the porch, steady and sure in his world. "I'll call Ottavio's," he called over his shoulder. "Paolo will hold a table for us."

❋ ❋ ❋

That evening, sitting in the park, Russell again felt glad to be breathing the air he knew: cool, dry, a good breeze gently blowing the treetops. Perfect kite-flying conditions. He opened a can of beer and handed it to his sister. He and Anita sat on the grass, waiting for Carl to launch his kite.

"Should we make a toast?" Anita called.

"Better say a prayer for this kite to go up," Carl returned with a laugh.

Carl took several quick strides, the wind picked up behind him, and the line went out. The kite bucked in the air, dipped, then swerved. The wind gathered beneath its orange-and-purple wings, and then it went up, up, furiously at first and then finally finding a comfortable spot in the sky. Carl hooted and gave them a thumbs-up. The kite turned and looped. Russell was up on his feet; he felt elated too. He also had something to do with it. It was his little secret. It would remain so.

Horse, Rope, Mud, Rain

Ann idled with the girls under cover of the white barn. She suspected Mr. Ray would be late because the rain had softened the cracked dirt road into thick putty. Rain pummeled the roof. Ann kept watch, leaning against the tack-room door. Nicki puffed on the cigarette they had stolen from Mr. Ray's desk, and Celia reclined in an empty wheelbarrow with her legs dangling over the edge, her black rubber boots swinging back and forth, back and forth.

Suddenly, Mr. Ray's voice called out through the pounding rain, "Ann, get the ropes!"

The three girls ran out of the barn, dragging long lead ropes through the mud. Ann hadn't realized the Appaloosa had been cast; he was writhing on his back, his legs caught under the bars of the corral. She glanced at the other girls guiltily. The sky hung like a sheet of aluminum foil over the red and white barns, the small arena dotted with rusted barrels and wood chicken coops.

"Nicki, hold the gate!" Mr. Ray shouted, standing in the muddy corral. "Celia, get the front leg."

Ann's fingers worked the slipknot. The horse thrashed his legs against the bars. Mr. Ray moved toward the frightened animal, who grew still and blinked his startled eyes free of rain, the whites flashing. Mr. Ray threw the loop around his front left leg. The horse flinched and kicked a hind leg against the pipe.

"Easy," Mr. Ray coaxed. Rain dripped off the rim of his hat. His hooked nose was an irritated shade of red, his blue lips pursed tightly. "Celia, get the other leg. Where's Page?"

Ann stayed silent, even though she normally spoke for the group. She pictured Page's defiant face in the barn, which smelled of damp sawdust and echoed the sound of horses chewing hay.

"Tomorrow," Page had said, "I'm not coming to work, because I've decided to sleep with Larry Dunbar." Ann's eyes had opened wide. Page often said things for effect, her free and unfiltered way of talking good for both admiration and laughs. But Larry Dunbar? She couldn't be serious. The girls had had so many conversations beneath the barn's rafters. Fear of high school, the man in the rain-coat who had flashed them in the drugstore, but losing your virginity to a guy like Larry Dunbar? Page couldn't be telling the truth.

"You're bluffing," Nicki said, breaking the silence. Nicki was one year older but pretended a lifetime of experience over the others. She did this, the other girls discussed, to compensate for the all-girls Catholic school she was forced to attend, dressed in uniform, her blond hair neatly bobbed. When Nicki listened to their stories of life in public school, a wave of longing swept across her face. Her mother had arranged for her to work at the stables to see if she'd tire of horses before she agreed to buy Nicki one.

Page shook her head defiantly. *No*, that shake declared, *I'll be the first to go all the way with Larry Dunbar, whether you like it or not.*

Rubber boots popped through the wet muck. Ann's faded jeans were spotted darkly with rain. She wore her dad's old green windbreaker, which hung to her knees, and had pulled her long hair through a rubber band she'd found at the bottom of her mother's coupon drawer.

Ann had worked at the stables the longest, for two years, since she was twelve. She took to the dirt and sweat naturally, glad when she was not anywhere else, not at school or at home with her two older sisters, who spent hours fixing their hair and playing with makeup. Her sisters said she'd soon tire of horses and working outdoors, but that hadn't happened yet. She hoped it never would.

Celia approached the horse, holding the rope tightly as she carefully avoided his hind leg. Ann knew her friend was scared. Frightened horses were unpredictable, quick to kick out in any direction. Rain trailed down the creases of Celia's tan slicker. Her hair was burnt orange and frizzy, wrenched into two tortoise combs that by afternoon weakened under the strain and sprang. One weekend morning, riding their bikes to the stables as the dew lifted, Celia had confessed that she liked a boy in their class but didn't think she had a chance with him. For days after, Ann kept an eye on Celia, anxious that her best friend might be fading away. She noticed Celia's gaze floating toward the boys, and how she would arrange herself in an oddly longish way, like a cat on a sunny windowsill. Celia tried to straighten her hair one day, coming to school looking nothing like herself, staring sheepishly through the pressed orange curtain as if she didn't know who it belonged to. Ann launched into suggestions for weekend trail rides in an attempt to recover her friend, secretly counting the days till summer, when they could be at the stables all day long, uninterrupted by school or boys, and meander on horseback through sage and creeks and live oaks, with nothing but backpack lunches and time on their hands.

Celia reached through the corral bars and threw the rope at the hoof, catching the corner of the iron shoe. Mr. Ray knocked the loop over the hoof, and she quickly tightened the rope around the horse's pastern.

"Not Dunbar!" Nicki had said that day in the barn.

Square jaw and wavy shock of thick, dark hair, Larry Dunbar accented his looks with rugged hiking boots laced in red. When he came to the stables, he'd coast his motorbike past the white fencepost so he wouldn't spook the horses or, more important, raise the ire of Mr. Ray.

Celia stared up at the rafters. She had never told the girls she liked Larry Dunbar, but Ann had seen her face when she learned he'd come to the stables for Page, not for her. She had looked surprised and crushed at the same time, a double emotion Ann could compare only to giving back a first-place ribbon mistakenly awarded.

"I would've picked someone better than Larry Dunbar!" Nicki said when Page left for the red barn. Ann wondered who that would be among the lunchroom filled with pleated navy skirts.

"What's wrong with Larry?" Celia shot out from her seat in the wheelbarrow. Sawdust clung to her orange hair.

"He's a goon," Nicki said, with all the authority she could summon.

Ann remembered the time she and Celia had sat bunched together beneath the chicken coop that was used for a jump. In the arena, a woman who had recently brought her horse to board at the stable rode around and around, oblivious to their presence in the coop. She was a serious woman who rarely acknowledged them, rendering herself prime material for unmerciful teasing when she used a section of garden hose for a crop. She clipped her horse's long mane so that it stuck straight up like a zebra's. When she rode, her legs dangled far below the horse's barrel, her toes pointed at the ground. It was a Saturday afternoon, her day to practice jumping. The girls watched through the wooden slats, giggling, as she adjusted her hard hat and flicked her horse's haunches with the makeshift crop.

"She looks like Sancho Panza," Celia had whispered.

Their plan had been to sneak inside the coop, wait for the horse to approach, and make a riot of noises that would spook him, cause him to refuse the fence, and send the woman with her garden hose sailing over the horse's head. Ann and Celia trembled with excitement. The horse thundered toward them, and they could see only its hooves, nostrils, and heaving chest.

They hadn't counted on the fear. Ann pictured the coop smashing to bits. Wood. Nails. Body parts. They held their breath but couldn't prevent themselves from looking. The hooves rose. Sand sprayed the wood. Grains struck them in the eyes as the horse and woman sailed above them. Later, the woman's boyfriend came to the stables and the girls watched speechlessly as the pair rode double uphill, bareback.

"He's not a goon," Celia said, ending the conversation.

Now, writhing on his back, the Appaloosa stared wildly at the dark sky. "Your turn, Ann," Mr. Ray said. She approached the horse, speaking in an even, low tone, coaxing the animal to accept her presence, her hands. Celia's voice softly joined Ann's as she stretched through the bars for the left hind leg, careful to keep out of striking distance of the other hind leg, which Page would have roped.

The horse's hind legs were covered in mud up to his hocks. An ugly horse—Roman nose and short barrel. Ann tossed the loop at the horse's upturned hoof and missed. The rope dragged across the mud. She moved closer.

"Get back," Mr. Ray called. He spoke sharply, the same way he spoke to Mr. Linnelman, who delivered three tons of alfalfa pellets to the silo, or Juan and Miguel, who trailered horses to the county fair.

Mr. Ray had hired the girls for minimum wage and free hours of riding. It was work usually reserved for laborers, and he expected no less from them. The girls knew little about Mr. Ray: an old man who managed the stables and, unless it rained, never arrived a minute late.

When Mr. Ray was young, the blacksmith once told them, he had been a real cowboy on the Montana plains. A real cowboy? Ann had wondered. One who branded with hot irons and broke wild colts? Ann had studied him carefully one day—his stooped shoulders, sparse gray hair, receding lips—and decided that the blacksmith had surely lied to them.

Ann drew back, holding the rope secure around the horse's hind leg. Ann, Celia, and Mr. Ray acted fast now, before the horse could panic. Ann folded the hind leg down like a hinge, almost to the bottom of the lower bar. Together they pulled the horse toward them, keeping the ropes low.

The horse wrenched onto his side, scraping his hard hooves against the belly of the aluminum pipe with a clatter. They pulled. The horse resisted. Ann's arms trembled. Then the horse balanced himself on one knee, the rope slackened, and Celia was sent crashing against the fence.

The horse heaved like a mountain pulling up from the earth. Celia scrambled to her feet, rubbing her elbow that had hit the pipe.

"You okay?" Ann shouted through the rain. She cursed Page under her breath for not being there.

"I'm all right," Celia said. She left the stall covered in mud.

Ann patted the horse's shoulder while Mr. Ray slipped the ropes off his legs.

"Stupid animal," he said.

The girls ran out of the rain, their hair and clothing drenched. Inside, the tack room smelled of dust and leather soap. Outside, a horse banged its trough against the corral pipe. Rain pelted the tin roof. They dried each other's hair with a towel that smelled of liniment. They went back over the event in detail—what they thought, where they stood, what they did—like survivors of a great adventure that involved danger and luck, life and death. Horse, rope, mud, rain.

"Lot of water in that stall." Mr. Ray walked into the tack room. He took off his hat and swiped his hand across his forehead. By now, the girls understood his indirect speech. He was uncomfortable expressing concern they knew he felt, so he rarely made eye contact.

"I'm okay," Celia said.

He stood by the door and stared out at the hill that turned solemn green when it rained. Trails cut across the hill's face. They turned a deeper brown. The landscape took on a richer hue than when the sun was out.

"I hate when it rains this much," he said. "My wife always wants me back early because she can't drive in it."

The girls were silent. They hardly ever heard him talk about his wife and couldn't imagine Mr. Ray with a private life outside the stables.

"The horses fed?" he asked over his shoulder.

"We're going." Ann pulled the damp towel from Celia.

"Where's Page?" he asked again.

No one spoke for a minute. Then, "She's late," Ann said.

She pictured Page in summertime—the sky clear and infinitely blue, the dirt road dry and cracked. She was wearing a cotton tank top that hung low on her chest. She had been the first to wear a bra. Ann hoped she would never need one herself. She had no wish to grow the bumps and curves her older sisters suffered.

Page had confided that Larry Dunbar had been trying for weeks against the cold tile in the school bathroom—*Oh, public schools!* Nicki's mind echoed—and once right here in the field, near the busted tractor with tires like pontoons. "I almost let him do it there," she said, "near that old tractor. But then I thought I could do better than Dunbar."

Page had assigned the time and the place. They would meet at her house. Her dad was away at work, her mom and brother visiting a college until Saturday. She and Larry Dunbar would meet right on the couch her mother meant to reupholster.

"That old couch?" Nicki said, incredulous. She spoke as if she'd have chosen a more romantic place, yet the girls knew she wouldn't have a clue.

After school. Three o'clock. Page had scheduled it like a driver's training course. "Cover for me," she had said, "if I'm late for work."

"She didn't come with you?" Mr. Ray asked.

Ann glanced at Celia. "No," she said. "Not today."

Mr. Ray scraped his muddy boot along the edge of the concrete step. "How does she plan to get here?"

Ann paused. She hated Page for making her lie. "Her brother's giving her a ride," she said.

✕ ✕ ✕

The rain stopped. The horses had been fed. Mr. Ray checked his watch and locked the tack-room door. He didn't say a word as the girls put their rakes in the shed and left.

Ann, Celia, and Nicki walked the back path toward the main road, where their rides would pick them up. They climbed over the rusted wire fence and dodged pits of mud.

Celia was silent. Nicki pulled a dry branch behind her, making a sloppy trail in the mud.

"I guess Larry Dunbar's happy," Nicki said. She laughed awkwardly. "Didn't think it'd take all afternoon."

"What do you know?" Celia shot back. She rubbed her elbow, which promised to bruise purple the next day. Ann knew she blamed Page for the bruise. "You don't know if she's still with him."

"Where else would she be?"

Celia didn't answer. She looked down at her muddied boots.

"I'm not going to lie for her again," Ann said. In the two years she had worked for Mr. Ray, she'd never lied to him once. He'd given her the job when he knew she was short of thirteen. He'd hired her friends.

Mr. Ray had chased Larry Dunbar off the stable premises twice last week. He said no one without horse business belonged there. Ann had pretended to be as critical of his actions as the rest of the girls were, although she had actually been relieved.

"I thought she'd come to help us feed," Nicki said. "At least that. I didn't think she'd take the whole afternoon. Didn't she say she'd come back and tell us all about it?"

No one answered. They kept walking the muddy path. *I won't lie another time*, Ann repeated to herself.

The girls walked by the old farmhouse that had been deserted for years. Last summer, they had opened its back door and roamed its cool, empty rooms, its creaking floors. They turned the faucet handles to watch rusty water flow. They imagined what it would be like to live in the farmhouse so close to the stables and decided that when they were old enough, they would buy it, fix it up, and live there together, alone.

"I bet Page will call him her boyfriend now. Can you see them? Page and Dunbar? Weird."

"What do you know?" Celia said. "You don't know what she'll do."

"I just said I *bet*." Nicki dropped her stick and bent down to scoop a handful of mud from a pit. She rolled it into a loose, globby ball. "What's the matter with you?" she asked playfully. "Sounds like you've got a crush on Dunbar."

She threw the ball, and it splattered across Celia's rear. Nicki laughed hard.

Celia pushed her to the ground in an instant. Nicki stuttered, and pain crossed her eyes. Celia mashed Nicki's neat blond hair into the pit and smeared mud on her face and neck. She felt none of the playfulness of rainy seasons past.

Ann grabbed Celia's shoulder. "Cut it out!" she yelled.

Celia didn't listen. She sat on Nicki's stomach, bearing down with all her weight. She scooped heaping palmfuls of mud and splashed them across Nicki's arms, neck, and legs.

"Get off!" Nicki shouted.

Ann threw her arms around Celia's shoulders. With all her might, she pulled her off and they toppled over, lying in another pit of mud.

"Damn it!" Ann cursed.

Celia moved off Ann, rubbing her sore elbow. Nicki stood apart from them. She spat dirt from her mouth. "What's the matter with you?" Nicki asked.

Celia rose and picked up a stick to scrape the mud off her pants. Ann sat in the mud, looking at her two friends. "Just great," Ann said.

Celia reached out a hand to Ann and pulled her up.

"Why'd you push her down?" Ann asked.

"I don't know," Celia said. "I just felt like it."

"You're crazy!" Nicki yelled. "You pushed me over Dunbar!"

"Forget about it!" Ann snapped. They were covered in mud, from their boots to their heads. They walked stiffly. Their clothes felt slack and heavy. Ann took off her windbreaker and tied the sleeves around her waist.

At the base of the path, Nicki's mother pulled up in her white Lexus. Her mother frowned when she saw them. "How am I supposed to drive you home like that?" She pulled a blanket from her trunk and draped it across the back seat. "You two need a ride?"

"No, Mrs. Witkin. My dad's coming to get us," Ann said.

Nicki slid onto the blanket and worked to close the door without smearing mud on the car.

"See you tomorrow," Ann said to Nicki.

"Sure," Nicki said. "Keep her away from me."

The sky darkened. It began to rain again. It was light at first, then stronger.

"Come on," Ann said. They walked to a felled eucalyptus tree. Its enormous trunk gaped, its insides rotting to dust. They huddled in its hull, protecting themselves from the downpour. It smelled of mint and damp bark.

"Do you think she really did it with him?" Celia asked after a while.

"I don't care if she did," Ann said. "But she better be here tomorrow. We'll probably have another horse caught. You know how they love to roll in the mud."

Celia didn't say anything, her mind somewhere else. Ann remembered the time they had gone on a trail ride to Wildwood Park, traveling in single file until they had reached a swollen reservoir and decided to cross it. The water had risen higher and higher, over their horses' legs, to their round barrels, and higher, to the tops of the girls' boots. Then they'd been weightless. Ann had felt no ground beneath her, no horse's hooves secure on the earth. She'd felt her horse swimming. Gliding. Celia had been as surprised as she was. Her face had broken into a smile.

"No," Ann said, realizing as she said it that it wouldn't make a difference. Her friend was already gone. "I don't think they have." She watched the rain pelt down. She picked up a piece of bark and tossed it into the wet air.

Acknowledgments

For early encouragement and tireless reading, I'm indebted to Justin Sherman, Tony Sanders, and Nicholas Delbanco. Thank you to my artistic collaborator and friend Cathryn Mezzo, who designed this beautiful cover, and to my role model Sharon Michaels, who never gives up.

Special thanks to the team: Brooke Warner, Shannon Green, Annie Tucker, Tabitha Lahr, and the indefatigable Elysse Wagner.

To Tim Sullivan—my husband and the true source of my "modern" family—and Matthew, Jack, Meghan, Lauren, and Catherine: I love you.

About the Author

Linda Feyder is a practicing psychotherapist in New York. She received her MA in creative writing and literature from the University of Houston, and has been writing fiction for many years. Her stories have appeared in literary journals and magazines. Her interest in California, her native state, and the people it attracts are the subjects of her debut collection of short stories. She lives in Long Island, New York, with her husband and enjoys traveling, visiting art museums, listening to other people's stories, and trying to learn French. Visit her online at www.lindafeyder.com.

Author photo © Marina Tychinina

SELECTED TITLES FROM SHE WRITES PRESS

She Writes Press is an independent publishing company founded to serve women writers everywhere. Visit us at www.shewritespress.com.

On Tràigh Lar Beach by Dianne Ebertt Beeaff. $16.95, 978-1-63152-771-5. Borne by the Gulf Stream, thirteen curious objects are tangled in the flotsam on the Hebridean beach of Tràigh Lar in Scotland. Erica Winchat, a young writer struggling with the stresses of a book contract, discovers them and tells the intriguing story behind each in her diary.

Our Love Could Light the World by Anne Leigh Parrish. $15.95, 978-1-938314-44-5. Twelve stories depicting a dysfunctional and chaotic—yet lovable—family that has to band together in order to survive.

True Stories at the Smoky View by Jill McCroskey Coupe. $16.95, 978-1-63152-051-8. The lives of a librarian and a ten-year-old boy are changed forever when they become stranded by a blizzard in a Tennessee motel and join forces in a very personal search for justice.

The Rooms Are Filled by Jessica Null Vealitzek. $16.95, 978-1-938314-58-2. The coming-of-age story of two outcasts—a nine-year-old boy who just lost his father, and a closeted young woman—brought together by circumstance.

The End of Miracles by Monica Starkman. $16.95, 978-1-63152-054-9. When a pregnancy following years of infertility ends in late miscarriage, Margo Kerber sinks into a depression—one that leads her, when she encounters a briefly unattended baby, to commit an unthinkable crime.

Profound and Perfect Things by Maribel Garcia. $16.95, 978-1-63152-541-4. When Isa, a closeted lesbian with conservative Mexican parents, has a one-night stand that results in an unwanted pregnancy, her sister, Cristina adopts the baby—but twelve years later, Isa, who regrets giving up her child, threatens to spill the secret of her daughter's true parentage.